MANDIE
AND THE
HIDDEN
TREASURE

Mandie Mysteries

1. *Mandie and the Secret Tunnel*
2. *Mandie and the Cherokee Legend*
3. *Mandie and the Ghost Bandits*
4. *Mandie and the Forbidden Attic*
5. *Mandie and the Trunk's Secret*
6. *Mandie and the Medicine Man*
7. *Mandie and the Charleston Phantom*
8. *Mandie and the Abandoned Mine*
9. *Mandie and the Hidden Treasure*
10. *Mandie and the Mysterious Bells*
11. *Mandie and the Holiday Surprise*
12. *Mandie and the Washington Nightmare*
13. *Mandie and the Midnight Journey*
14. *Mandie and the Shipboard Mystery*
15. *Mandie and the Foreign Spies*
16. *Mandie and the Silent Catacombs*
17. *Mandie and the Singing Chalet*
18. *Mandie and the Jumping Juniper*
19. *Mandie and the Mysterious Fisherman*
20. *Mandie and the Windmill's Message*
21. *Mandie and the Fiery Rescue*
22. *Mandie and the Angel's Secret*
23. *Mandie and the Dangerous Imposters*
24. *Mandie and the Invisible Troublemaker*
25. *Mandie and Her Missing Kin*

Mandie's Cookbook
Mandie and Joe's Christmas Surprise

MANDIE
AND THE
HIDDEN TREASURE

Lois Gladys Leppard

BETHANY HOUSE PUBLISHERS
MINNEAPOLIS, MINNESOTA 55438

Mandie and the Hidden Treasure
Lois Gladys Leppard

Library of Congress Catalog Card Number 87–71606

ISBN 0-87123-977-9

Published by Bethany House Publishers
A Division of Bethany Fellowship, Inc.
6820 Auto Club Road, Minneapolis, Minnesota 55438

Printed in the United States of America

With Thanks to

W. Harold Christian, Jr.,
who has so many talents and
who so willingly shares them.

"For unto whomsoever much is given, of him shall be much required." Luke 12:48

About the Author

LOIS GLADYS LEPPARD has been a Federal Civil Service employee in various countries around the world. She makes her home in South Carolina.

The stories of her own mother's childhood are the basis for many of the incidents incorporated in this series.

Table of Contents

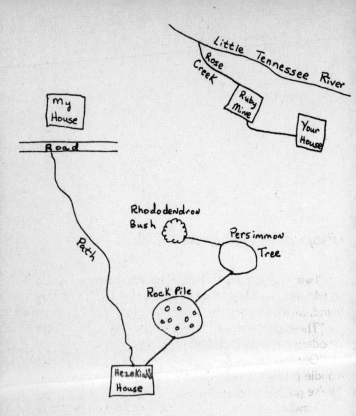

Go down the path to Hezekiah's House. Turn left and go 936 feet to Rockpile. Go right 572 feet to Persimmon Tree. Then go left 333 feet to Rhododendron Bush. Dig three feet under Rhododendron Bush. That is where Treasure is buried.

Drawn by Ruby May Shaw
April 30, 1850

Chapter 1 / The Treasure Map

"I wish Celia and Dimar could have stayed and helped us find the treasure," Mandie said as she and her Indian friend, Sallie, climbed the steep stairs to the attic.

"There might not be any treasure, you know," Joe Woodard reminded her, following close behind.

"Oh, Joe, you know there's some kind of treasure," Mandie protested as they reached the top of the stairs. "We've got the map to prove it."

Snowball, Mandie's white kitten, ran ahead of them as Mandie pushed open the door to the attic.

The three stepped over crates and trunks and made their way through a maze of abandoned chairs, dressers, and other discarded furniture to get to the huge old wardrobe standing at the far side of the attic.

"Just because we found a map is no reason to say there really is a treasure," Joe argued. "Someone might have found it a long time ago. That map's about fifty years old. By now, someone could have taken whatever was there."

Mandie bent to open the big drawer on the bottom of the wardrobe and took out the treasure map they had found a few days earlier. As they sat down on the floor of the attic, she spread the map out before them.

"I'm going to look anyway," Mandie told him. "Since Ruby got killed the day after she drew this map, I don't imagine she took the treasure out of its hiding place. And since we found the map tacked to the back side of that old sideboard, I don't believe anyone else ever found it."

"I think as you do, Mandie," Sallie said. "We must explore the places shown on the map and see what we can find."

"Oh, I'll go along with you girls and help look, but I really don't think there will be anything to find," Joe said.

Mandie ignored his remark this time. She read the directions on the map. "It says, 'Go down the path to Hezekiah's House. Turn left and go 936 feet to Rock Pile. Go right 572 feet to Persimmon Tree. Then go left 333 feet to Rhododendron Bush. Dig three feet under Rhododendron Bush. That is where the Treasure is buried." Mandie looked up. "I'm sure Ruby buried something," she said emphatically.

Joe leaned forward, pointing to the drawing. "We've already decided the 'My House' on the map must be this house we're in," he said, "because Ruby was your father's sister, and this was your grandparents' house. Then there is a path drawn to 'Hezekiah's House' right there."

"And we go 936 feet to a rock pile, 572 feet to a persimmon tree, and 333 feet to a rhododendron bush," Sallie added, studying the map.

Mandie nodded. "There's the Little Tennessee River, the ruby mine, and a place marked 'Your House.' It's all right here in Franklin, North Carolina," she said. "But I don't know anything about that path that goes to Hezekiah's House."

"I don't think we can begin in the middle or at the end of this map," Joe told them. "We'll have to start at the beginning and find the path to Hezekiah's house. It looks to me like that path must go right next to the cemetery across the road from here."

"Yes, it does," Mandie agreed.

"The 'Your House' might be the old house where Jake and Ludie Burns are living now," Sallie suggested.

"It probably is," Mandie agreed. "And if it is, then this rhododendron bush, the persimmon tree, and the rock pile must be between our house and the house the Burnses are living in."

"Well, we're not going to find it sitting here in the attic," Joe told the girls.

Mandie picked up the map and turned the front of it around to show Joe and Sallie. "Don't y'all think these things are between here and the Burnses?" She glanced down at the back of the paper map. "Wait! Here's something on the back. Look!" She laid the map upside down for the others to see. "I believe it says, 'It's about'—something—" She shook her head. " '—to Hezekiah's House.' "

" 'One mile,' " Sallie filled in, squinting closely at the writing.

"So it's about one mile to Hezekiah's house," Joe agreed. "Do y'all see anything else written on the back?"

The three of them carefully inspected every inch of the faded paper but found nothing else.

"I guess we've got all the information there is on the map," Mandie sighed. "What do y'all suppose the treasure is?"

"Some silly kid thing," Joe said. "Ruby was only ten years old when she drew this map."

"Lacking five days," Mandie corrected him. "She was

born May 6, 1840, and she died on May 1, 1850, five days before her tenth birthday, according to her tombstone."

"Oh, well, nine years and three hundred and sixty days if you want to be exact," Joe grumbled.

"Ten years old is not such a dumb age, Joe," Mandie said. "I'm only twelve myself, and you're not quite two years older than I am."

"And I am almost one year older than you, Mandie," Sallie added. "My grandfather said that Ruby was a sensible, mature little girl. I think she probably hid something valuable."

"It might have been considered valuable by a ten-year-old," Joe said.

"Maybe it was money," Sallie suggested.

"Or jewelry," Mandie said. She lifted the map from the floor, and a small fragment fell off the corner where the tack had made a hole. "This map is so old it is beginning to crumble," she said, pointing to the corner.

"Then we must hurry and find the treasure," Sallie said.

"Where do we begin?" Mandie asked the others.

"We should find the path by the cemetery," Joe stated.

"Or we could talk to my grandfather," Sallie said. "He was living here then with your grandparents, remember?"

"Let's do both," Mandie agreed, getting up from the floor. "Let's find your grandfather and see what he knows, and then we can go to the cemetery across the road." As she held the map, another corner crumbled from the paper.

Sallie gasped. "The map is disintegrating!"

"Why don't we make a copy and put this one back in the drawer?" Mandie suggested. "If this falls apart before we find the treasure, we might not be able to piece it together again. Joe, you can draw better than I can. Will you copy it for us?"

Joe smiled. "Where is the pencil and paper?"

"I'll run down to my room and get some. I'll be right back." Mandie handed him the map and wove her way through the old furniture again.

On the way down the stairs, Mandie met Sallie's grandfather coming up the steps. "Uncle Ned, I'm glad you're coming up to the attic. We have lots of questions we want to ask you," she told him. "I have to go to my room for something. I'll be back up in a minute. Sallie and Joe are up there now."

Uncle Ned smiled at the blonde-haired, blue-eyed girl and continued his way up. "I wait in attic, Papoose."

Mandie rushed into her room, grabbed paper and pencil from her desk, and ran back up the steps, close behind the old Indian. "Here, Joe," she said, holding out the supplies.

"I'll draw right here," Joe said. He knelt to use the top of an old trunk for a table and spread out the map and his supplies. Snowball hopped upon the trunk to watch. "Sit down, Snowball," Joe ordered him. The kitten perched on the edge of one corner.

"Joe is making a copy of the map because the old one is crumbling," Mandie explained to Uncle Ned. "You might as well sit down because we've got lots of questions to ask you."

Uncle Ned smiled and sat on top of another old trunk nearby. Mandie and Sallie sat down on a dusty, faded settee near him.

"Now, Papoose, question," the old Indian said.

"Did you ever know of anyone named Hezekiah?" Mandie asked.

"Hezzie—ky?" the old man asked, unable to pronounce the name. "No, Papoose, I not know."

"Look here on the map." Mandie jumped up and pointed over Joe's shoulder. "You see, it says, 'My House' there, and then it shows a path to Hezekiah's house. It goes across the road, and it must run right next to the cemetery. Do you know if there's a path like that?"

Uncle Ned shook his head. "Not know, Papoose. May be. Not remember."

Sallie moved closer. "My grandfather, do you know whether the 'Your House' on the map is the same house the Burnses live in?"

"My granddaughter, people live in that house long ago, work for father of John Shaw in mines, plant crops. Same house Jake Burns live in now," Uncle Ned replied.

"Who were they, Uncle Ned?" Mandie asked eagerly.

"Not remember." The old Indian frowned for a moment as if trying to recall. "Man called Scoot," he said after a moment.

Joe looked up from his drawing. "But why would Ruby put that house on her map?"

"Daughter of Scoot same age Ruby. Good friends. Ride ponies together," Uncle Ned told them.

"Then I'd say that whoever the girl was, she must have known about Ruby's map and probably about the treasure, too, whatever it is," Mandie said.

"Yeh, and she could have dug it up years and years ago," Joe reminded her.

Uncle Ned shook his head. "No, no, no. Mine close when Ruby die. Scoot move far away."

Mandie looked down at the map Joe was copying. "What about all these other things—the rock pile, the persimmon tree, and the rhododendron bush?" she asked. "Do you know where they are?"

The old Indian laughed and said, "Papoose, on this land find many, many trees, bushes, rocks."

"If we only knew where Hezekiah's house was, then we could count the feet from there," Sallie said.

Just then Mandie looked up. There in the doorway stood Polly Cornwallis, Mandie's next-door neighbor. Polly's long, dark hair was neatly tied back with ribbons, and she was wearing an expensive-looking pink silk dress.

"Hello, everybody," Polly greeted them. "Mandie, your mother told me y'all were up here looking for treasure."

Mandie sighed. "No, Polly," she replied, "we are not looking for treasure up here. We have an old map we found that we're trying to decipher."

Polly squeezed through the furniture maze to look over Joe's shoulder. He looked up at her without speaking, then continued drawing.

"That map?" Polly questioned. "Hey, that looks awfully interesting. Can I help y'all find the treasure on it?"

The other three young people looked at each other.

Mandie hesitated. "Sure, Polly, but I warn you. It may be a tiresome, dirty job, and I know you don't like to get dirty."

"Oh, that's all right. I don't have anything else to do until I go back to school Monday," Polly told her, smoothing her fancy dress.

Mandie caught Uncle Ned's eye and he smiled. Mandie smiled back. Uncle Ned knew Mandie didn't especially like Polly because Polly was forever trying to be too friendly with Joe. He also knew it had taken a lot of self-control for Mandie to include Polly in the treasure hunt.

"You must go home and put on an old dress," Sallie

told Polly. "We will be searching through weeds and bushes."

"Never mind about my dress. If I ruin it, I have lots of others," Polly said, twirling her full skirt. "When do we start?"

"You mean *where* do we start, Polly," Joe said. He turned to Mandie. "How *are* we going to get started on this silly adventure, anyway?"

"It's silly, is it? Then why did you beg your parents to let you stay over the rest of the weekend to help Sallie and me look for whatever this treasure is?" Mandie asked.

Joe grinned. "Because I have to be here to get you out of all the silly messes you get into."

"Joe Woodard!" Mandie exclaimed. "I can take care of myself!"

"But it always helps to have a boy along," Sallie spoke up. "Remember, Mandie, we have met up with some dangerous people before."

Polly gasped. "Are there any dangerous people involved in this search for the treasure?"

"Who knows? We don't even know how to start on this yet," Mandie said. "If we only knew who Hezekiah was and where he lived. . . . Uncle Ned, is there anybody still living around town who was here back then?"

Uncle Ned thought for a moment. "Me, Morning Star live in this house with father of John Shaw. Long ago. Long, long ago."

Polly looked at the map again and saw the date. "April 30, 1850!" she exclaimed. "My goodness! You mean the map is that old? Why, my mother wasn't even born then!"

Mandie told her all about finding the map tacked to the back of the sideboard, where it had been hidden all these years.

Then Uncle Ned continued his recollections. "People named Massey live in house next to father of John Shaw."

"My house," Polly agreed. "And my mother bought the house from them after my father died. I was just a little baby then."

"What happened to them? Are they still living in Franklin?" Mandie asked.

The old Indian shook his head. "No, move way up north."

"Is there no one at all in Franklin who lived here back then?" Mandie asked.

"Hadleys," Uncle Ned said. "Hadleys live here then. Same house they live in now. Papoose go see Hadleys."

"The Hadleys? Where that strange girl Hilda ran away to? Away over beyond the ruby mine?" Joe asked.

Mandie shot Joe a look of disapproval for talking that way about the disturbed young girl Mandie and her friend Celia had found hiding in the school attic.

Uncle Ned nodded. "Yes," he replied. "Maybe Hadleys know this Hezzie—ky for you."

"I know where they live. May I go with y'all?" Polly asked quickly.

"I know where they live, too," Joe replied. "I've been there with my father when he had to doctor them for one thing or another."

"When are you going?" Polly was insistent.

"Whenever my mother gives us permission, Polly. Don't you ever have to get permission from your mother to do things like going on this search with us? Your mother might not want you to do that." Mandie secretly hoped that Polly would not be allowed to go.

"No, most of the time Mother lets me do whatever I want," Polly said. "She says I'm growing up and should learn to make decisions for myself. I don't think she'll mind if I go with y'all."

"You will have to ask her first, Polly. We don't want you going off with us unless your mother agrees," Joe spoke up.

"I'll ask her. Just tell me when you're planning to go," Polly said.

"I'll let you know. Right now, Joe has to finish copying the map before we can go anywhere," Mandie told her.

A moment later, Joe stood up, waving his new map in the air. "Here it is. All done."

Mandie and Sallie looked at it and agreed he had done a good job.

Carefully picking up the old map, Mandie returned it to the drawer in the bottom of the wardrobe. "Uncle Ned, are you going with us to the Hadleys?" she asked.

"We see," the old man said, standing up.

"Please do, Uncle Ned," Mandie pleaded, taking his old wrinkled hand in her small white one. "Remember, my mother said I couldn't go anywhere without an adult for the rest of my holidays at home because I disobeyed her and got in trouble at the mine."

Uncle Ned smiled down at her. "We see, Papoose."

"Must be time to eat. I'm hungry," Joe said.

Sallie laughed. "You are always ready to eat, Joe, whether it is time or not."

"It's about noon," Polly said. "I'll go home and eat, and ask my mother if I can go with y'all. Then I'll come back and let you know. You won't go until I get back, will you?"

"Not if you don't take too long," Mandie told her. "I'll ask Mother if we can go just as soon as we eat. We're going to the Hadleys first of all. And Polly, please wear something sensible."

"All right. I'll hurry," Polly called back. She ran out the door and disappeared down the steps.

"Let's go," Mandie said, picking up Snowball and leading the way down the stairs. "I suppose we'll have to eat since Joe is hungry."

In the parlor they found Elizabeth, Mandie's beautiful, blonde-haired mother, and John Shaw, Mandie's uncle, who had married Elizabeth after Mandie's father died.

Uncle John laughed when he saw them. "I knew you'd be along soon," he said. "The wonderful aroma from that chicken Jenny is frying is all over the house."

"Fried chicken!" Joe exclaimed. "Mmm!"

Uncle Ned sat down near John Shaw while the young people gathered on the settee.

"Have you figured out the map yet?" Elizabeth asked.

"Some of it, Mother," Mandie replied. "Uncle Ned said we should go talk to the Hadleys to see if they know who Hezekiah was and where he lived."

"Why the Hadleys, Amanda?" Elizabeth asked.

"They're the only people Uncle Ned can think of that were living here when Ruby made the map," Mandie explained.

"And we need to ask them some questions," Joe put in.

"Amanda, you know I told you that you couldn't go off anywhere without an adult with you. Who is going with you?"

"Me go," Uncle Ned volunteered. "Me go with Papoose after eat."

"We'd appreciate that, Uncle Ned," John said. "I know

we can always depend on you to keep things under control."

"Like when John Shaw little brave." The old Indian's black eyes twinkled.

"Yes, like when I was little," Uncle John agreed. "You did a good job of looking after me and my brother, Jim, when we were growing up. I don't know what we'd have done without you and Morning Star to get us out of our scrapes." He chuckled.

"John and Jim not bad braves," Uncle Ned replied.

Mandie went over and gave her old Indian friend a hug. "Thank you, Uncle Ned, for saying you'll go with us," she said. "We'll be good and not get into any trouble. I don't know about Polly, but the three of us will behave."

"Polly? Is she going with y'all?" Elizabeth asked.

"If her mother lets her," Mandie said with a big sigh. "I just wish we could have slipped off without her finding out what we're doing. She's not much fun to be around."

"Amanda!" Elizabeth scolded.

Liza, the young Negro maid, appeared in the doorway. Elizabeth looked up. "Yes, Liza?"

"Dat Missy Polly, she done sent huh cook over heah to say wait fo' huh 'cause huh ma say she kin go," Liza announced.

"Thank you, Liza." Elizabeth smiled. "They'll wait for Polly."

"Yessum," Liza replied, still standing in the doorway. "And Miz 'Lizbeth, Aunt Lou she say de dinnuh on de table."

As they rose and went to the dining room, Mandie whispered to Sallie, "We'll just have to pretend Polly's not there."

"That may be hard to do," Sally whispered back.

Chapter 2 / Old Newspapers

Jason Bond, the Shaws' caretaker, had ponies saddled and waiting for the young people at the gate when they finished their noon meal. Uncle Ned's horse was also at the hitching post.

As the young people gathered in the front hall, preparing to leave, Mandie stood in front of the mirror on the hall tree, tying her bonnet.

Suddenly Polly burst through the front door. "I made it!" she exclaimed, out of breath. "And I tied my pony out in front with the others."

Mandie silently looked the girl over. At least she had changed into a gingham dress and was carrying a bonnet and a shawl.

"Mandie, Sallie, take these." Elizabeth handed them the shawls from the pegs on the hall tree. "It's cool outside. And remember, Polly, you must obey Uncle Ned the same as the others have promised."

"Yes, ma'am," Polly agreed. She looked at Mandie. "Who's got the map?"

"I have it," Joe called to her from the doorway as he buttoned his jacket. He held up the rolled-up piece of paper for her to see.

Uncle Ned came into the hallway wearing his buckskin jacket and headed for the front door. "Go!" he said.

Amid reminders from Elizabeth and John Shaw to behave, the young people rushed down the walkway to their ponies.

When Mandie got to the gate, Liza was standing there, waiting for her. Taking Mandie by the arm, she whispered, "Hurry, Missy, git on yo' pony and git 'side dat doctuh son. Dis heah Missy Polly, she got eyes fo' him."

Mandie mounted her pony. "I know," she said with a sigh.

As the group headed out, Mandie tried to ride beside Joe, but Polly kept crowding the road with her pony, and Mandie would be forced to hurry forward toward Sallie and Uncle Ned.

Sallie dropped back to ride beside Mandie. "If the Hadleys did know Hezekiah, what will we do next?" she asked, trying to distract Mandie from watching Polly.

"I hope they remember Hezekiah. Who knows? Maybe we could find him and talk to him. He must have been a friend of Ruby's, don't you think?"

"He probably was," Sally agreed.

"If we hurry, maybe we can find the treasure before we have to go back to school. I wish I didn't have to keep going to that silly school in Asheville," Mandie said.

"But your mother went to the Misses Heathwood's School for Girls, and she wants you to get educated there also," Sallie reminded her.

"They'll never educate me—not what I call educate. They teach so many silly things that I will never use. I'd like to learn mathematics and finance like the boys do. That would be more useful to me when I grow up," Mandie said as they rode along behind Uncle Ned.

"I do not know where you can learn those things except at a boys' school, and I do not think they would allow you to attend there." Sallie giggled. "I agree that you should learn mathematics and finance because some day you will inherit your uncle's and your mother's fortunes. But then most girls just get married and let their husbands worry about that kind of thing."

"Not me," Mandie said quickly. "I would want to know what goes on in my own business affairs. No man is going to tell me how to spend my money when I grow up."

"Not even Joe?" Sallie teased.

Mandie hesitated. "Not even Joe," she said uneasily. "But I don't think Joe would be like that when he grows up. He always treats me like an equal. He encourages me to learn sensible things."

Mandie turned slightly on her pony to look over her shoulder. Polly was riding close beside Joe and seemed to be doing most of the talking.

Looking back at her friend, Mandie said, "Besides, who knows how the future will turn out. Joe and I may outgrow each other some day."

"Yes, you are right," Sallie agreed. She changed the subject. "Are we almost to the Hadleys?"

"It's not much farther," Mandie said, tightening her grip on the reins. "Let's get ahead of Uncle Ned. I know the way."

"But my grandfather is supposed to be watching over us," Sallie objected.

"We'll stay within sight of him. Let's just ride ahead." Mandie urged her pony past Uncle Ned, and Sallie followed.

The old Indian raised his hand to them. "Do not go far ahead," he called.

"We won't," the girls called back.

As they rounded a bend in the road, the Hadleys' huge two-story house came into sight. Everyone hurried forward.

They tied up the animals at the hitching post and rushed to the front porch. Mandie knocked, and a moment later the door was opened by a uniformed maid.

"Are Mr. and Mrs. Hadley at home?" Mandie asked the woman.

The maid looked over the group standing on the porch and asked, "Who is calling?"

Mandie waved her hands around to her friends and replied, "I'm Mandie Shaw. This is Joe Woodard and that's Uncle Ned and Sallie and Polly."

"Just a moment," said the woman and disappeared inside. She returned in a minute and showed them into the parlor where Mr. and Mrs. Hadley were sitting.

Mr. Hadley rose slowly and stepped forward to offer Uncle Ned his hand. "How are you, Uncle Ned?" he said. "I see you have brought us some company." The two men shook hands.

"Papoose of Jim Shaw want to ask questions," Uncle Ned said, taking a seat indicated by Mr. Hadley.

Mr. Hadley spoke to Mandie. "So you are Jim Shaw's daughter. He was a good man, my dear. A good man." He put his arm around Mandie's shoulders.

"Thank you, sir." Mandie's voice trembled. "I'm so glad to finally get to meet you and Mrs. Hadley."

"Sit down. Sit down. Make yourselves at home," Mrs. Hadley told them.

The young people found seats around the room, and Mandie told the Hadleys about her father's sister, Ruby, and the treasure map she had left. She showed them the copy of the map that Joe was carrying.

The Hadleys listened attentively.

"What we would like to know, Mrs. Hadley and Mr. Hadley, is whether you all were living here back then," Mandie said.

"Yes, my dear, we were here," Mrs. Hadley answered. "I was born and raised in this house, and after my parents died, I married Mr. Hadley. And we've continued living here ever since. I have never lived anywhere else."

"Did you know Ruby Shaw?" Joe asked impatiently.

Mrs. Hadley nodded her head slowly. "Yes, we knew Ruby. We were just a young, newly married couple when that terrible accident happened. Mandie, your grandparents suffered so much, especially your grandfather. He would never allow anyone to mention Ruby's name after she died. He could not bear to talk about it."

"If you were living here then, did you know someone named Hezekiah who lived in that house on the map?" Mandie asked.

Mr. and Mrs. Hadley looked at the map again. They thought for a moment.

"Hezekiah?" Mr. Hadley mulled over the name.

"I can't figure out where that house would be, dear," Mrs. Hadley said.

Joe leaned forward. "Did you ever know anyone at all named Hezekiah?" he persisted.

"I don't believe so," Mr. Hadley answered.

"No, I'm sure I never knew anyone with that name," Mrs. Hadley said.

The young people sighed in disappointment.

Uncle Ned frowned thoughtfully. "Map say Hezzie— ky not far from house of John Shaw." He bent forward to point at the place on the map.

"About one mile, according to the back of the original map. This one is a copy that Joe made because the other one is crumbling," Mandie explained.

"I am sorry, dear," said Mrs. Hadley, "but I just can't seem to place this house on the map. I didn't know your grandparents well."

"I have an idea that might help," Mr. Hadley offered. "I used to own the local newspaper. When I retired a few years ago, I just closed it down. Someone else started the newspaper we have now. But there are hundreds of old newspapers in my old building. They date back to about 1845. Maybe you could find some kind of information in them, at least the story about Ruby's death."

"Oh, could we look at them?" Mandie said excitedly.

The other young people leaned forward.

"All I ask is that you don't take any papers out of the building, and that you leave them as you found them," Mr. Hadley said. "I'll go get the key. Uncle Ned, you know where the building is, I'm sure."

"Yes," the old Indian agreed.

Mr. Hadley went to get the key, and when he returned, he handed it to Uncle Ned. "I'll trust you to return it to me when they're finished looking."

"Thanks so much, Mr. Hadley and Mrs. Hadley," Mandie said, rising to go.

The young people all expressed their thanks.

Mrs. Hadley hobbled to her feet with her cane and raised her hand to them. "Wait!" she called. "There is one promise I'd like from y'all."

Everyone turned to listen.

"Promise me you'll let me know what the treasure is when you find it. This is something I would like to have done when I was your age," she told them. "It sounds so exciting."

"We promise," the young people said in unison.

The Hadleys followed them to the front door.

"Good luck!" Mrs. Hadley called with a twinkle in her eyes.

The young people excitedly mounted their ponies and waited for Uncle Ned to catch up with them.

"Can we go there right now, Uncle Ned?" Mandie asked excitedly.

Uncle Ned untied his horse, smiled, and looked at the sky. "We have time," he replied.

"Thank you, Uncle Ned, for helping us and everything," Joe said.

The old Indian smiled again. "Must hurry before doctor son get hungry."

Everyone laughed as they rode off down the road toward the downtown part of Franklin.

On Main Street Uncle Ned stopped in front of an old two-story building, badly in need of paint. A rotting sign over the doorway with fading letters read: *Franklin News*.

The young people jumped down and tied their ponies at the edge of the road alongside Uncle Ned's horse. Then they followed him to the front door of the building.

After much turning and shaking, Uncle Ned finally got the door unlocked and pushed it open for the young people to enter. "I wait here," he told them, sitting down on the front step.

As they went inside, they looked around the dark, dusty hallway. Long-unused printing presses stood in a large room with dirty windows on their right. On the left was a room stacked almost to the ceiling with newspapers. One large window high in the wall dimly lit the room.

At the back of the hallway, a long flight of steps led upstairs.

Mandie surveyed the piles of newspapers. "What a mess!" she exclaimed.

Joe walked over to the papers and looked for dates on them. "I don't think these are very old," he said.

"Let's see what's upstairs," Mandie suggested, heading up the steps.

Joe followed, the rickety boards creaking at every step.

Polly shrank back. "Are y'all really going up those dark steps?"

"Come on, Polly," Sallie said, offering her hand.

Polly reluctantly gave Sallie one hand and held up her long skirts with the other. They slowly climbed the dark stairway.

As they came to the landing at the top, Polly shivered. "There may be rats in here," she said.

"If there are, they will be frightened of us and run away," Sally assured her.

The upstairs was one big room, almost completely filled with copies of old newspapers. The only light for the room came from a large skylight covered with grime.

Mandie and Joe looked about and began searching for dates on the papers. Sallie let go of Polly's hand and joined them.

"We are looking for 1850 newspapers," Mandie said. As she pulled the top paper off one stack, a cloud of dust assailed them, and Polly backed off, sneezing.

Over in one corner, Sallie began reading dates aloud. "This says 1845, these are 1849, and these are 1845 again."

As they explored the stacks and moved the papers

about, the room became clouded with dust. Their hands got black with newspaper print, and dirt settled in their hair and on their clothes. Polly stayed at the top of the stairs, watching the others and holding her handkerchief to her nose.

"Here they are!" Joe called from the far side of the room. As he attempted to pull out a newspaper sticking out of a huge stack, the entire pile came tumbling down on top of him, sliding this way and that.

Rushing to see what Joe had found, Mandie and Sallie got caught in the avalanche of newspapers. As they looked at each other among the mountain of papers, the three suddenly laughed hysterically and then started sneezing from the dust.

"You're all dirty, Mandie," Joe told her as he worked his way out of the mess.

"So are you, Joe," Mandie said.

"We are all a mess!" Sallie gasped, trying to help Joe extricate himself from the newspapers.

"Remember, Mr. Hadley said to leave the papers as you found them," Polly reminded them as she watched from the top of the steps.

The other three looked at each other in exasperation.

"How can we ever get those papers back like we found them?" Mandie asked.

"We don't know what order they were in when they fell," Joe remarked.

Sallie picked up a few of the papers in front of her. "I think if we just stack them neatly, it will be all right," she suggested.

"Good idea, Sallie. That's all we can do," Mandie agreed.

"But we'd better read as we stack," Joe warned. "Otherwise, we'll have to take the stack apart again."

"Let's just sit down here and look through them." Mandie plopped down in the middle of the scattered papers and picked up one issue at a time.

"I can't find the 1850 copies I spotted before the pile fell in," Joe murmured as he continued shifting papers.

"Here is one dated the week of Monday, March 4, 1850," Sallie said.

Mandie looked up. "See if you can find one for later. Ruby died May first, remember?"

"We should stack the papers as we look at them, to get them out of our way," Sallie said.

"Right!" Joe agreed.

Mandie pushed the fallen papers away from the corner. "Let's make a pile right here." She began a new stack with the paper she had just checked.

"Are y'all going to read all those dirty old newspapers?" Polly called to them, keeping her distance.

"Maybe. Don't you want to help?" Joe asked.

"No, thank you. I'm dirty enough from all the dust y'all stirred up," Polly answered, still holding her handkerchief over her nose and mouth.

As Mandie looked over at Polly, she noticed a door near where Polly was standing on the landing. "Hey, Polly!" she called. "Open that door behind you and see what's in there."

Polly quickly turned around. She looked at the door with the ceramic doorknob and shrank away from it. "No!" she cried. "It's—it's probably—dark in there, whatever it is."

Sallie jumped up. "I will open it."

As Sallie approached, Polly moved down a couple of steps, away from the door. Mandie and Joe watched across the room as Sallie tried to push the door open. When it finally gave way, there was a terrible noise from inside the room. It sounded like someone beating on things and throwing things around, and there were creepy moans among it all.

Joe and Mandie raced to Sallie's side as she stood back, afraid to enter the room.

"It's dark as pitch in there!" Joe exclaimed.

"What is all that noise? I can't see a thing," Mandie cried.

"It's probably rats," Joe decided.

"Rats do not whine like that," Sallie protested.

"Hand me that yardstick over there. I'll poke it inside," Joe told the girls.

Mandie got the yardstick and handed it to Joe. He gradually pushed the stick inside the dark room. Then getting braver, he stepped one foot inside and whacked the yardstick around, hitting something and causing a greater commotion.

Mandie, standing close behind him, jerked back. "Something cold touched my head!" she cried.

Joe backed out with her, but when he did, something touched his head also. Reaching up to fight it off, whatever it was, he realized he was banging at a chain dangling from above. He pulled hard on it, and suddenly the room was flooded with light.

Looking up, they saw an old skylight opened by the chain. At the same instant, there was a great fluttering sound and dozens of birds flew out the opening. It was just an empty room with one small, dirty, broken window.

"Pigeons!" Mandie gasped.

"What a relief!" Joe exclaimed.

"We should have recognized their sound," Sallie said.

Polly, still watching from the steps, called to them. "At least it wasn't rats."

At that moment a huge field rat ran out of the room, scurried past Polly within inches of her feet, and disappeared into a hole in the floor.

Polly screamed, grabbed up her skirts, and ran down the stairs. She ran all the way out the front door and joined Uncle Ned to wait for the others.

The other three young people laughed until their sides hurt.

"We'd really better get busy," Mandie finally managed to say. "Uncle Ned will be saying it's time to go home pretty soon."

Sallie and Joe agreed.

In a short time Mandie had located the newspaper for the week of Monday, April 29, 1850. "This is the paper for the week Ruby died," she said excitedly. Sitting in the middle of the floor, she spread the paper out as Sallie and Joe joined her.

They read the whole eight-page paper but found nothing at all about the Shaws or anyone named Hezekiah.

"Wait. We are looking at the wrong paper," Sallie told them. "If Ruby did not die until May first, it would not have been in this newspaper at all. It would be in the one for the next week."

"That's right, Sallie," Mandie said.

Joe scrambled for more papers, and in a few minutes he had located the one for the week of Monday, May 6, 1850. He laid it out on the floor before them.

The three anxiously combed the pages of the newspaper and finally found an account of Ruby's death.

Mandie read aloud with a quiver in her voice. " 'Little

Miss Ruby May Shaw, nine-year-old daughter of John and Talitha Shaw, died Wednesday, May 1, evidently thrown from her pony near her father's mine. Mine workers say she was well and happy when she mounted her pony after a visit with them that day. A young Negro boy found her lying in the bushes halfway between the mine and her home. She was already dead. Her pony was grazing nearby. The town will mourn the loss of this bright, friendly little lady who knew no strangers. She was buried in the church cemetery on Thursday, May 2, across the road from her home. Today would have been her tenth birthday.' "

Mandie, Joe, and Sallie looked at each other.

"So sad!" Sallie whispered.

"Terrible!" Joe agreed in a husky voice.

Mandie wiped a tear from her eye. "I wish I could have known her," she said.

"I wonder who the Negro boy was. They don't even give his name," Joe puzzled.

"Maybe my grandfather knows," Sallie suggested.

"Let's get these newspapers stacked back up so we can leave," Mandie said.

Soon everything was back in shape. They looked around, closed the skylight in the empty room, closed that door, and hurried downstairs to find Uncle Ned.

The old Indian was sitting alone on the front step.

"Where is Polly?" Mandie asked, looking about.

"Home," Uncle Ned replied. "Her cook come down road in wagon. Polly get her pony and follow home."

Mandie breathed a sigh of relief.

"Papooses all dirty," Uncle Ned said as he stood up to survey the group. "Doctor son, too." He shook his head slowly. "Mother of Papoose not like dirt."

The three young people looked down at themselves guiltily.

Joe shrugged. "We found the newspaper with the story about Ruby's death in it. It was near the bottom of a huge pile, and when I tried to pull it out, everything caved in on top of me," he explained. "And the girls got dirty trying to help me get out."

Uncle Ned just shook his head again.

"The newspaper said a young Negro boy found Ruby lying in the bushes after her pony had thrown her," Mandie said. "Do you remember who he was?"

"No, Papoose," Uncle Ned answered. "I in Deep Creek, doing business things when Ruby die."

"Didn't anyone ever discuss it or say anything about the boy afterward?" Joe asked.

"Father of Ruby Shaw not allow it. Family, servants, not speak of it ever," the old Indian said.

"But I imagine people in town talked about it, didn't they?" Joe asked.

"Yes, there was much talk. But Father of Ruby know boy not guilty," Uncle Ned replied.

"Was the mine closed the same day that Ruby died?" Sallie asked.

"Yes. Father of Ruby say sad, bad mine," the old Indian said.

"Maybe the Hadleys would remember who the boy was," Mandie suggested. "They had the story in their newspaper. They must have known."

"No more today. Go home. Wash," Uncle Ned told them. Motioning for them to get on their ponies, he strode over to his horse and mounted.

"Will you go back to the Hadleys with us tomorrow, Uncle Ned?" Mandie begged. "Please!"

"We have to return the key to them anyway," Sallie reminded him.

"We could go with you when you return the key," Joe said.

"We see," Uncle Ned grunted.

"I hope they can remember who the boy was," Mandie said as they rode off toward home.

Chapter 3 / Cemetery Path

"Come in. Come in. Make yourselves at home," Mr. Hadley greeted the group the next morning, opening his front door wide.

"Morning," the young people chorused, following their host and Uncle Ned into the parlor.

"Thank you for key," Uncle Ned said, handing it to him.

"You are very welcome," Mr. Hadley replied. "Sit down. Sit down," he invited. "I am sorry Mrs. Hadley is a little under the weather this morning. Well, what did you find in the old newspapers?"

The three young people perched on a settee nearby.

"We thank you, Mr. Hadley, for letting us look at your old papers," Mandie said. "We found the story about Ruby's death. It said a young Negro boy found her after the accident. Do you remember who he was?"

"A young Negro boy?" Mr. Hadley repeated. He scratched his thick gray hair. "Well now, I don't believe I remember. In fact, I don't think anyone ever said who he was. He was probably just someone who happened to be passing by."

"Did the authorities investigate the accident?" Joe asked.

"I don't think so. You see, it was taken for granted that her pony had thrown her," Mr. Hadley explained. "Besides, as we told you before, her father wouldn't talk to anyone about it. Even the funeral was private."

"Do you know of anyone else who was living here when it happened, someone who is still living here in Franklin?" Mandie asked.

Mr. Hadley thought for a moment. "I don't believe I do. Most of our friends are dead now."

Sallie spoke up. "Is the funeral man still living?"

"The funeral man? Oh, the undertaker," Mr. Hadley answered. "Why, yes, I believe the current undertaker was in business back then, or at least it was the same family."

"Where is the funeral parlor?" Mandie asked.

"Right down on Main Street below our newspaper building. It's called *Hudson's Undertakers*," Mr. Hadley said. "I don't know whether they kept any records back then or not, but someone there might have some kind of information."

"Thank you, Mr. Hadley," Mandie replied as the young people rose to go.

"I hope Mrs. Hadley will be feeling better," Sallie said.

"We appreciate your help," Joe added.

Outside, as they mounted their ponies, Mandie spoke to Uncle Ned. "Mother won't let us go to the undertakers without an adult . . ." she began.

"It would only take a few minutes to stop by there, Uncle Ned," Joe said.

Sallie smiled as she watched her friends try to convince her grandfather to take them.

"Not this day," Uncle Ned insisted as they rode off. "Later."

When they arrived at Mandie's house, they hurried up the walkway in search of Uncle John. They found him in the library bent over a lot of papers on his desk.

"Uncle John," Mandie began as the young people gathered around him. "Uncle Ned can't go with us to the undertakers, and Mother won't let us go anywhere without an adult. Will you please take us?" she begged.

"The undertakers? What are you talking about?" Uncle John laid down his pen and straightened in the big chair.

Mandie quickly explained.

Uncle John shook his head. "I'm sorry, Amanda. I can't go anywhere today. There's a businessman coming to see me in a little while, and he'll probably be here all afternoon."

"Oh, shucks!" Mandie exclaimed.

"Why don't y'all go do something else for the time being? Go measure some of the distances on the map or something," Uncle John suggested. "But you must stay within sight of the house."

"That's a good idea," Joe said.

"I do have to get back to my work here," Uncle John said. "Maybe tomorrow I'll have time to help you."

The young people went outside and strolled across the road to the cemetery.

"Now how are we going to measure the distances? We don't have anything to measure with," Joe said as they stood at the iron gate to the cemetery.

"First, we should find the pathway next to the cemetery shown on the map because we'll have to measure from the house on down that pathway," Mandie said. "Or would you like to see Ruby's grave first?"

"Yes, let's do that. Come on," Joe said, lifting the latch to open the gate.

The girls followed him inside the walled-in cemetery, and they walked quietly among the tombstones.

"Here is Ruby's grave," Mandie said, kneeling by the broken tombstone. "You see, it's all cracked up with pieces missing. Uncle John is going to have it repaired if possible. If not, he's going to have a new one put up."

Joe pointed to a huge double monument nearby. "And here are your grandparents' graves," he said.

Mandie got up to look and then went on to the next plot. "And here are the graves of my great-grandparents," she said, stopping at the next two individual stones. "I wish my father had been buried here so I could put flowers on his grave." She looked up at Joe. "Do you ever go to the graveyard back home at Charley Gap?" Tears swam in her blue eyes.

Joe patted her hand. "I do, Mandie. Every once in a while I take flowers up there and put them on your father's grave, just like I promised."

"Thank you, Joe." Mandie cleared her throat.

"Do you not think your father would have rather been buried in the mountains he loved so much?" Sallie asked.

"I guess so." Mandie quickly changed the subject. "We need to find that path now." She started to leave, but Joe kept looking around.

"Hey, there's another gate!" he said excitedly, hurrying toward the back corner to investigate.

Mandie and Sallie caught up with him. The big iron gate was just like the one at the front.

Mandie stood on tiptoe to see over the wall to the outside. "There's a pathway outside!" she exclaimed.

"We've found it." She reached up to lift the rusty latch on the gate. It wouldn't budge.

"Let me try," Joe said.

"This latch must not have been used in a long time," Sallie observed.

"I'm afraid we're going to have to get a hammer or something to knock it open," Joe finally said.

"Let's just go around," Mandie suggested.

When they assembled again on the other side of the cemetery wall, Mandie looked down the faint path that seemed to start at the back corner of the cemetery. "This path is really overgrown. I didn't even know it was here," she said.

"Well, at least we found it," Joe remarked. "Now we must decide how to measure the distances on the map."

Mandie thought for a moment. "Let's go find Abraham and see if he has anything to measure with," she suggested.

They found the old Negro gardener working among the Shaws' beautiful flower beds.

"Abraham," Mandie began, "do you have anything we can measure with?"

Abraham stopped his work and leaned on his hoe. "What y'all want to measure?" he asked.

"We're hunting for buried treasure, and we've got a map and everything," Mandie said with a twinkle in her eye. She hoped he wouldn't take her seriously. She didn't want to have to go through all the explanations again.

"And how fur might dat be?" Abraham asked.

"About a mile or so," Mandie said.

"A mile or so," the old man repeated. "De longest measure I'se got be dat rope hangin' on de fence over dere. It be one hundred foot long."

Joe went to pick it up and said, "This is just what we need if you'll let us borrow it."

"Sho, go ahaid," the old man said.

"Thanks, Abraham. Let's start at our front porch," Mandie said, turning to lead the way. Then she stopped and turned back to the gardener. "Abraham, how long have you lived here?" she asked.

"I live here years and years, Missy," the old Negro said. His smile showed quite a few teeth missing.

"Were you living here in 1850?" Joe asked.

"In 1850? No, I guess not. My fambly moved to Noo Yawk City in 1847 when I be eight year old," the Negro said.

"But you came back sometime or other because you're here now," Mandie reminded him.

"Missy, I comes back when I be sixteen year old and go to work for yo' grandpa. Mistuh John, he be 'bout seven year old den," the old man explained.

Mandie quickly calculated the dates. "You came back about 1855 then?"

"I reckon. I don't knows, Missy. I'se born in 1839. I knows dat," the old man said.

"So you left in 1847 if you were eight years old. Did you know Mandie's grandparents before you moved to New York?" Joe asked.

"No, I'se a lil' child den. Didn't know much folks dat I kin 'member," Abraham replied. "My ma and pa die in Noo Yawk City. My uncle asks old Mistuh Shaw if he could hep me out. He kindly gives me work and a place to live back here in Franklin. Been here ever since."

"Guess we're out of luck there," Joe told Mandie.

"He couldn't have known Ruby, and he certainly

wasn't here when she died." Mandie turned to walk toward the porch. "Now, to get down to business. The map says it's one mile to Hezekiah's house."

"And there are 5,280 feet in a mile, so if we stretch the rope between us, and the last one keeps moving forward, it won't take long," Joe said.

"Yes, and we can do this standing up as we walk," Mandie agreed.

The old Negro gardener wandered over to watch them stretch the rope and move forward.

They were almost even with the back gate of the cemetery when they heard Liza calling. They looked up to see her standing beside Abraham at the front gate to the house.

"Eatin' time!" the Negro girl yelled. "Eatin' time!"

"Of all times to call us to eat!" Mandie sighed.

"We'll have to remember where we stopped, or we'll have to measure it all over again," Joe said.

"How many is that?" Mandie asked.

"Five rope lengths," Sallie announced.

"Right," Joe agreed. "That's 500 feet."

"But we still have a long way to go." Mandie sighed again.

"Eatin' time," Liza called again from across the road.

"Coming!" Mandie yelled as they started back.

When they came to the house gate, Liza asked, "What y'all be doin' by dat graveyard?"

"Dey's lookin' for buried treasure, Liza," Abraham teased.

"Buried treasure? Ain't no buried treasure in dat graveyard," she replied. "Nuthin' but buried daid folks."

"You're right, Liza," Mandie agreed.

"Come on. Time to eat," the Negro girl said as she turned to go back to the house. Looking back at the three straggling young people, she added, "Like Aunt Lou say, git a move on!" She danced on across the yard.

"I'll leave the rope on the fence, Abraham," Joe said as he draped it over.

Laughing, Mandie, Sallie, and Joe turned to say good-bye to Abraham. At that moment a horse and buggy pulled up at the hitching post, and they stopped to see who it was. Liza also stopped to watch.

A huge Negro man in a fine dress suit jumped down and spoke to the gardener. "Abraham, how are you?" he asked, holding out his hand.

Abraham's eyes grew big, and he reached to put an arm around the big man. "Samuel!" he cried. "Where y'all come from? Noo Yawk City a long way off from here!"

"I came to visit my brother. He's been under the weather lately, and I thought I'd better come down and check him over," the man said, glancing at the young people.

Abraham proudly turned to the young people and said, "I wants y'all to meet my very best friend from Noo Yawk City, Mistuh Doctuh Samuel H. Plumbley."

The three stepped forward to shake hands, greeting the man.

"I'm Mandie Shaw," Mandie said, introducing her friends, as well.

"How do you do, Missy?" the doctor replied. "Pleased to make your acquaintance, all of you."

"Glad to meet you," Joe said. "My father is also a doctor."

"Is that right? Does he live here in Franklin?" the man asked.

"No, we live over in Swain County in the mountains, but he doctors people all around," Joe replied.

"I'm glad to hear that there is a physician practicing around here," the doctor said.

Aunt Lou appeared on the front porch. "You younguns git in here!" she yelled across the yard. "Food's on de table, and you keepin' it waitin'."

Liza ran around the house to the back door to avoid Aunt Lou.

"Yes, Aunt Lou. We're coming," Mandie answered. She turned back to the doctor and said, "I'm glad to have met you, Dr. Plumbley, but we have to go eat now. Bye."

"Good-bye, Missy," the doctor replied.

The three rushed into the house, leaving Dr. Plumbley and Abraham standing in the yard.

"He sounds awfully educated," Sallie remarked.

"Yes, he does," Mandie agreed. "But then I suppose all the people in New York are educated. They have so much money up there that nobody should be poor."

"Oh, Mandie," Joe protested. "That's not so at all. Every place has its rich and its poor. You need to travel around the country and get better educated about these things."

"Just give me time, Joe Woodard!" Mandie snapped.

Chapter 4 / Abraham's Secret

"Uncle John, we met a doctor who is visiting Abraham," Mandie remarked as they all sat down to the noon meal.

"Doctor? What doctor? Is Abraham sick?" Uncle John questioned her.

"Oh, no. He's a friend of Abraham's from New York," Mandie explained.

"Yes, Abraham did live in New York years ago," Uncle John replied, passing the bowl of green beans to Joe.

"Abraham let us use his rope to measure the distances on the map," Joe said, helping himself to the beans.

"But we did not get finished," Sallie said.

"Because we had to stop and come and eat," Mandie added, reaching for a piece of hot corn bread.

"Measuring what?" Elizabeth asked.

"We've been trying to figure out some distances on the map Ruby made. And the path to Hezekiah's house, whoever he was, seems to go right next to the graveyard," Mandie explained.

"But, dear, if you don't know who this Hezekiah was

or where he lived, how are you going to find his house?" Elizabeth asked.

"I don't know, but we'll find it somehow because we have to count the feet from his house to other things on the map in order to find the treasure," Mandie said.

Uncle Ned was sitting near Uncle John. "Papoose will find. Always." He smiled.

"If you say we will, then we will." Mandie grinned at the old Indian.

Joe turned to Mandie. "I was just thinking," he said. "I wonder if Abraham's doctor friend ever lived here in Franklin."

"We didn't even ask, did we? Why don't we go find out?" Mandie suggested.

"What's the man's name?" Uncle John asked, sipping his coffee.

"Abraham introduced him to us as Mister Doctor Samuel H. Plumbley," Mandie replied, laughing.

"Plumbley? I don't believe I ever knew anyone here named Plumbley," Uncle John said. "Did you, Elizabeth?"

"No, that's not a familiar name," his wife replied. "What does he look like?"

"He's a big Negro man," Mandie said, "and real friendly."

"He is an older man, but not as old as my grandfather," Sallie added.

"A Negro man?" Uncle John asked. "Uncle Ned, did you ever know a Negro doctor here in Franklin?"

Uncle Ned shook his head. "No such doctor ever here."

"Come to think of it, he has a brother in town," Joe said. "He told us his brother had been sick, and he came down from New York to check him over."

"That's right," Mandie agreed.

"We should go ask Abraham more questions," Sallie said.

John and Elizabeth looked at each other, puzzled.

"Let us know what you find out," Uncle John told the young people.

"We will," Mandie promised.

As soon as they could finish the meal, the young people asked to be excused from the table. They hurried to the front door, and looked out at the gate to see if the horse and buggy were still there.

"Oh, he's gone!" Mandie whined.

"Let's go see Abraham anyway. Maybe he knows something." Joe led the way down the front steps and around the house to the gardener's cottage.

Abraham was sitting in a rocking chair on his front porch with a cup of coffee in his hand. The young people crowded around the chair.

"Where is your doctor friend, Abraham?" Mandie asked.

"Oh, he done gone back to his brother's house," Abraham said.

"Abraham, did your doctor friend ever live in Franklin?" Joe asked.

"Samuel? Why, he sho' did—"

Instantly Abraham was bombarded by questions from all three at once.

"Whoa, there! I ain't got but one set of ears. I cain't hear but one question at a time."

Everyone laughed.

"We're sorry," Mandie apologized. "When did he live here?"

"Well now, I reckon he lived wid his grandparents out

yonder in de country. Dey die and he go live wid kinfolks in Noo Yawk City," the old man explained.

"When did he leave Franklin? About what year?" Joe asked.

"Well, it's like dis here. My ma and pa, dey buy their freedom and move to Noo Yawk City to find work 'cause Samuel's kinfolks live up there and tell 'em 'bout it," Abraham began. "Den when I be 'bout thirteen year old, Samuel's grandma and grandpa dey die, and he come live wid kinfolks in Noo Yawk City near where we live."

"When were you thirteen?" Joe began figuring. "That would have been in 1852."

"In 1852!" Mandie repeated quickly. "Then he *was* here!"

"Yes, he would have been living here in 1850," Sallie agreed.

"Abraham, we've got to talk to him. Where does his brother live?" Mandie asked excitedly.

"His brother, he live 'bout ten mile from here," the old man said.

"Ten miles! Mandie, we can't go that far," Joe said. "Is he coming back to see you, Abraham?"

"He sho' is."

"When?" Sallie asked.

"Soon as he gits done doctorin' dat brother of his," Abraham assured them, taking a drink of his coffee.

"Do you think he might have known my grandfather?" Mandie asked.

"Yo' grandpa? Don't imagine so. I didn't know de Shaws 'til I comes back from Noo Yawk City. You see, me and Samuel, we's just younguns back den. We didn't know no grownup white folks," the old man said.

"You don't have any idea when Dr. Plumbley will be

back to see you?" Mandie persisted.

"Like I done tol' you, he come back when he git done doctorin' dat brother of his," he said. "Den y'all come back and talk all you wants wid him."

"Would you please knock on the kitchen door and ask Jenny to let us know when he comes back?" Mandie asked.

Abraham shook his head quickly. "No, Missy, I don't talk to dat Jenny."

"You don't talk to Jenny?" Joe asked. "What do you mean?"

"Well, it be like dis here," the old man explained. "'Bout forty year ago, me and dat Jenny, we gits hitched by de travelin' preacher. Den three days later I ketch her makin' eyes at dat Willie what work in de stables on Main Street, and I say to her, you gits out of my house right heah and now."

The young people listened, fascinated by his tale.

"And she got out?" Joe asked.

"She sho' did, bag and baggage," Abraham said.

"Where did she go?" Sallie asked.

"Why, Missy heah," he said, indicating Mandie, "her grandpa give Jenny a room up there on de third flo' of de big house where she been ever since."

"You mean you and Jenny have been married for forty years and haven't lived together but three days?" Mandie gasped.

"And you haven't even spoken to each other in all that time?" Joe asked.

"Dat's what I been tellin' y'all. Don't you listen to what I say?" Abraham rocked back and forth quickly in the rocking chair.

"You and Jenny must run into each other, living and

working around here," Sallie said.

Abraham looked out from the porch toward his beautiful flowers. "Jenny cook fo' de big house and live there. I garden de flowers and live out heah," he replied. "Missy's grandpa, he give me dis house fo' long as I live. We don't see each other. If we does, she run quick her way, and I goes quick my way."

"But Abraham, she's your wife. You must have loved her, or you wouldn't have married her," Mandie said.

"Jes' wife accordin' to de law only," Abraham said. "She don't love me. Never did. She go cuttin' eyes at dat Willie when our weddin' wuz jes' three day old."

"Has she been makin' eyes at that Willie all this time?" Joe asked.

"Nope. Dat Willie cut his eyes on another woman. He be married since four days after we did," Abraham said.

"This all sounds like you and Jenny just had some kind of misunderstanding," Mandie said. "Maybe you misunderstood things, Abraham, or maybe she did."

"I ain't misunderstood nothin'. I seed her and she ain't misunderstood. She gits out when I say git out," the gardener replied.

"But you said Willie got married four days after y'all did. If he'd been interested in Jenny, he wouldn't have married another woman, would he?" Joe asked.

"No matter what he innerested in. Dat Jenny got innerested in him after she done married to me," he insisted.

"Abraham, the Bible says we must forgive others for any wrong they do us," Mandie reminded him.

"I knows what de Bible say. I done read it cover to cover. But I ain't never goin' to fo'give her fo' actin' like dat.

"So y'all might as well go on back to yo' measurin'. Cain't nobody change my mind," the old man said as he rose from the rocking chair.

"How will we know when your friend comes back?" Joe asked.

"You kin git dat Mistuh Jason Bond to watch out fo' him. He let you know. Now go on back to yo' measurin'," he said, opening his front door to go inside.

"All right. I'll go ask Mr. Jason to let us know," Mandie said.

The gardener went inside the house.

"I'll go find Jason Bond and ask him. Wait here." Joe ran across the yard and through the back door of the house, then came running back a minute later. "I was lucky. He was in the kitchen. He'll watch for us. Let's go," he told the girls.

Mandie picked up a hoe leaning against the end of Abraham's porch.

"We might need this," she said.

"All right but it'll be a nuisance to carry along," Joe said, as he took the rope from the fence where they had left it.

They hurried across the road to continue measuring.

"Do you all believe Abraham told us the truth?" Sallie asked as they approached the cemetery.

Joe and Mandie stopped to look at the Indian girl.

"The truth?" Joe asked.

"About what, Jenny or the doctor?" Mandie asked.

"I think the truth is that Abraham still loves Jenny, and all these forty years he has not known how to tell her so," Sallie answered.

"I sorta thought that, too," Joe said.

"Do you think Jenny still loves him?" Mandie asked

as they walked on toward the spot where they quit measuring.

"I do not know Jenny well," Sallie replied.

"I know she cooks wonderful food, and they say the way to a man's heart is through his stomach," Joe said, laughing.

"Abraham doesn't eat her cooking," Mandie reminded him. "He lives all alone in his house and does all his own housekeeping, and cooking, and everything. But if Jenny has never been interested in another man in all these years, I'd say she still loves him. I have an idea. . . ."

"No interfering with other people's quarrels!" Joe warned.

Mandie put her hands on her hips. "I'm not planning to interfere, Joe Woodard! You could at least let me finish before you jump to conclusions. I was going to suggest that we talk to Aunt Lou about Abraham and Jenny. She has been here forever, and she would know everything."

"What good would that do?" Joe asked. "We are not going to butt into other people's business!"

"There's no harm in finding out all the facts," Mandie retorted.

Sallie spoke up. "I would like to know more about it. It is too bad if two people are in love and stay apart because of anger."

"All right, you girls talk to Aunt Lou. I won't have anything to do with it. I'll just keep measuring." Joe leaned against the wall at the back corner of the cemetery. "Are you two going to help or not?"

"Of course we're going to help. You're not going to find the hidden treasure all by yourself," Mandie told him.

"This is where we stopped," Sallie said, patting the corner of the brick wall with the palm of her hand. "We had already measured five hundred feet from the porch to here, remember?"

"Yes, and we have just 4,780 feet left to make a mile," Joe replied.

"Do you still have the map in your apron pocket, Mandie?" Sallie asked.

"Yes, but it seems like that path curves around behind the cemetery. Once we get back there, we'll be out of sight of the house. Uncle John warned us to stay within sight of the house unless an adult is with us. I'll run ask my mother if Liza can come."

"Liza's not an adult! She's only a couple years older than you are," Joe reminded her.

"We've run out of adults right now," Mandie argued. "Maybe my mother will let Liza come since no adult is available. I'll be back in a minute." She ran toward the house, disappearing inside the front door.

Elizabeth, who was walking down the hallway at the time, turned to see who was coming through the front door in such a big hurry. "What's wrong?" she asked quickly.

"Nothing, Mother," Mandie said, breathless from running.

"I came to ask you if Liza could go with us on down the path behind the cemetery. We'll be out of sight of the house then, and all the grownups are busy."

"Down the path behind the cemetery?"

Mandie pulled the map out of her pocket again and showed her mother where they had been measuring to find the path to Hezekiah's house. "We've measured all the way to here, and we need to measure on down the pathway that goes behind the cemetery," she explained.

"What do you want with Liza?" Elizabeth asked.

"We just wanted her to go with us in place of an adult, so you'd let us go on with our search," Mandie said. "Please, Mother."

"Every time you get out of my sight you get into trouble, Amanda," Elizabeth replied.

"I promise I'll behave and won't get into anything bad. Please, Mother. Time is running out. We all have to go back to school next week," Mandie pleaded.

"I know that," Elizabeth replied. "Do you promise to obey Liza?" she asked. "I'll caution her to keep you in her sight."

"Yes, ma'am. I promise. I'll do whatever you say."

"All right, let's find her. I think she's in the kitchen." Elizabeth turned down the hallway.

Mandie followed. "Thank you, Mother."

Elizabeth explained to Liza that she was to go with the young people and make sure they did not get out of her sight. Liza didn't like the idea much until she found out they didn't have to go *through* the cemetery.

Liza stepped into the pantry and took down a large container of cookies from a nearby shelf. Opening it, Liza started rolling up some of the cookies in a dish towel.

"What are you doing?" Mandie asked.

"We's got to have some food for tea time. I'll jes' stick some of dese in dis towel and bring 'em along," Liza told her. "You go on now. I'll meet you outside in a minute."

"All right, but hurry. We'll be at the back gate."

"I'se on my way, Missy," Liza replied.

"But where is Liza? Isn't she going with us?" Sallie asked, as Mandie caught up with her and Joe.

"Here she comes," Mandie said, watching the Negro girl run out of the house, swinging the towel tied in knots to hold the cookies.

"Where we goin', Missy?" Liza asked as she approached.

"Down this way." Mandie pointed down the dirt pathway ahead of them. "Now we have to measure how long it is, so you'll have to help us count."

"I don't know how to measure," Liza protested.

"We'll do the measuring. You just carry the hoe," Joe said.

"How much y'all gwine t' count?" Liza took the hoe.

"Four thousand, seven hundred and eighty feet," Joe replied. "But we've already got a good start."

"Lawsy mercy, dat's gwine t' take all day and all night!" Liza exclaimed. "Good I brung dese heah cookies." She patted the towel.

"Oh, good! Food!" Joe laughed. "But we have to work first."

"It goes fast, Liza," Sallie told her.

"Anyway, we have to be back in time for supper," Mandie said.

"I gits out of heppin' dat Jenny cook de supper! Ha! ha!" Liza laughed, merrily dancing around.

As they stretched the rope, Mandie asked, "Liza, what is Abraham's last name?"

"Abraham? Why, he be known as Mistuh Davis," Liza replied, looking at Mandie curiously. "Why you want to know dat, Missy?"

"Davis," Mandie repeated. "Liza, did you know that Jenny and Abraham are married—"

"Mandie!" Joe interrupted. "You're starting something!"

"No, I'm not," Mandie said, turning back to Liza. "They've been married forty years. Did you know that, Liza?"

"Lawsy mercy! No, Missy. Who say dey married?" Liza asked, her black eyes growing round in amazement. "I ain't never heerd dat."

"Abraham told us," Mandie said.

She explained the story to Liza as they began moving forward with the rope.

"Well, bust my buttons! Ain't dat a crazy tale!" Liza exclaimed. "I always wondered why dat Jenny ain't never been sweet on no man. Now I knows. She sweet on Abraham!"

"Do you think so, Liza?" Sallie asked.

"I knows so," Liza said. "I ain't never seed dat woman even look at another man in my life, and I'se almos' fifteen years old."

"Are you sure, Liza?" Mandie asked.

"I knows everything dat woman does. She cook, wash dishes, eat, and sleep. She don't go nowheres, not even to church wid de rest of us. And she save ebry bit o' dat money what yo' uncle pay her to work."

"Does Abraham go to church with y'all?" Mandie asked.

"He sho' do, every Sunday, and sometimes fo' prayer meetin'," Liza replied.

"Then that's why she won't go—because he does," Mandie said.

"Oh, come on, Mandie. Pay attention to the measuring, or we'll never get done," Joe said.

The narrow path wound through bushes and weeds. It was hard work but they continued on. After measuring four thousand feet they rounded a bend and came to a dead end. The trees and bushes before them were so thick that there was no sign of the path continuing.

Mandie looked around. "Don't tell me this is the end!"

"I can't see any more of a path," Joe said.

"Remember, it has been about fifty years since Ruby made that map. Trees and bushes grow big in that length of time. They may have completely covered the path," Sallie reminded them.

Liza plopped down on a nearby log. "Lawsy mercy, Missy!" she exclaimed. "I'se tired. Ain't y'all? Let's jes' git a lil' rest and have our tea time." She unrolled the towel.

The others joined her on the log and sat munching on the cookies Liza had brought.

"What are we gwine t' do after we runs out of cookies?" Liza asked.

"We're going to have to search the woods all around here to find the path," Joe replied.

"And it's going to be an awful job trying to measure through all that stuff growing around here," Mandie added.

"We can do it," Sallie said confidently.

But Mandie was not so sure about that.

Chapter 5 / Fine Food Since 1852

As soon as the last cookie crumb was swallowed, the young people were ready to continue their search for the rest of the path.

"Sallie, you know more about this kind of thing than we do. Tell us how to go about finding the rest of the path," Mandie asked her friend.

"If there is any more of it," Joe added.

"Yes, there was more at one time," Sallie said, peering through the bushes. "You see the shortest, youngest trees and bushes there. Those have grown up since the other ones that were already along the side of the path."

"I see what you mean. If the path was not used, and trees and things grew up in the middle of it, they would all be smaller and newer than the others," Mandie said.

Joe was poking among the bushes, bending things this way and that in order to look about underneath.

"I see a lot of small rocks and gravel under this bush," Joe said, bending things out of his way.

Sallie came to look. "You are right. That is part of the path."

Joe began beating the bushes with the hoe to clear the path.

"Y'all gwine t'walk through all dat stuff?" Liza asked, watching Joe.

"We have to follow the old pathway, or road, whatever it was," Mandie told her.

"I ain't so sho' I'm gwine t' follow y'all," Liza replied.

Joe was several feet into the bushes when he called to them. "Hey, this goes into a clearing. Come on."

Sallie immediately followed him, but Liza stayed back. Mandie turned to her. "Come on, Liza," she said.

"Y'all go ahaid. I'll jes' wait here fo' you," the Negro girl replied.

"No, you have to go with us," Mandie said. Stepping back to take the girl's hand, she pulled her forward. "You promised my mother you would stay with us. Remember, you got out of helping Jenny cook supper by coming with us."

"But I didn't bargain for no wilderness like dat," Liza protested, trying to pull her hand free.

"If you don't come with us, Liza, we'll all have to go home. Please come," Mandie pleaded.

Sallie stepped back out of the bushes. "Come on, Liza. Look, Joe has already made a path through there. You can see through to the clearing on the other side. Come on." She bent the remaining bushes back so Liza could see.

Liza peered ahead and finally allowed Mandie to hold her hand. Mandie slowly urged her forward. As they got to the middle of the broken down bushes, a playful squirrel romped through underfoot. Liza screamed and rushed forward to where Joe was standing in the clearing.

"What happened?" Joe asked the girls.

"Nothing. A squirrel ran through and brushed against our legs," Mandie explained.

Liza held her sides in fright. "Dat wudn't no squirrel. Dat be a snake."

"No, Liza. I saw it," Sallie said. "It was a squirrel."

"Let's git goin' befo' it come back," Liza said, walking forward down the open pathway. "I ain't used to no sech things. I stay home where I belongs. I don't go trampin' 'round de world like y'all does."

"I'm sorry," Mandie said, catching up with the girl.

"You jes' go yo' way. I'se stayin' up here next to de doctuh son. He protect me."

"Wait a minute," Joe said. "We've got to measure the distance through the bushes I chopped down."

They backtracked enough to add the distance to their calculated total while Liza, shivering with fright, stood in the opening, waiting.

All of a sudden something white came bouncing out of the bushes and rubbed around Liza's ankles. She screamed, and the others came running.

"Snowball! Where did you come from?" Mandie rushed forward to grab her kitten. "Look, Liza, it's only Snowball. Look."

The Negro girl finally hushed and opened her eyes. She stared at the white kitten. "You mean dat Snowball come runnin' over my feet?" Liza asked shakily.

"That's right. Here he is," Mandie said, rubbing the kitten's fur.

"How he git here?"

"I don't know. He must have been following us all the way here," Mandie replied. "Do you want to carry him for me?"

Liza took the kitten and cuddled him in her arms. "Snowball, you bad kitten, scaring lil' ol' Liza like dat," she scolded.

Snowball purred and reached up to lick her throat.

"That cat!" Joe said, exasperated.

"Joe, you know he always goes with me everywhere," Mandie said. "This time I left him in the house because I didn't want to have to stop measuring to go find him when he decided to run off."

"He got out somehow," Joe said. "Maybe he'll keep Liza entertained so she'll quit that screaming every time we turn around."

Sallie looked ahead. "It looks like the path goes on out of sight without anything else blocking it."

"Let's work fast while the path is clear," Mandie said, as they moved forward with the rope stretched between them.

They walked on quickly down the path without finding any more obstructions. Then suddenly they came to the end of it.

"The path ends up at that main road ahead. Look!" Joe quickened his strides.

In seconds they all stood on the main road.

"Look!" Mandie pointed to a big house directly in front of them across the main road.

"How many feet have we gone now?" Sally asked.

"A little more than 5000 feet," Joe calculated.

"Then that must be Hezekiah's house," Mandie cried. "Come on. Let's go over there!"

They ran across the road and stopped at the edge to look at the house. There was a sign across the front door: *Fine Food Since 1852.*

"A restaurant!" Mandie exclaimed.

"Probably a boardinghouse," Joe said.

"It has been in business since two years after Ruby died," Sallie noted.

"Don't look like no bidness to me. Look like somebody's house," Liza muttered, holding Snowball tightly.

"Let's go knock on the door," Mandie suggested.

They walked up the long front yard, and as they approached the porch, two people came out the door.

As the door swung open, Joe peeked inside. "Looks like a store inside to me. I don't think we should knock. You don't knock on a store door. You just go in," he said, pushing the door inward.

The girls followed close behind. The inside did look like a variety store, but there was also the strong, wonderful aroma of food cooking.

"Food!" Joe whispered.

The girls smiled at him.

Behind a counter stood a short, fat, bald-headed man, and Joe led the way toward him.

"How do you do, sir?" Joe began, introducing himself and the others, including Snowball.

The man looked up and smiled. "What can I do for y'all?"

"We're looking for a house where a man named Hezekiah lived about fifty years ago," Mandie said.

"Fifty years ago? Hezekiah?" the man asked in amazement.

"Yes, sir. How long have you lived here?" Joe asked.

"We've been here about thirty-five years," the man said.

"Thirty-five years," Sallie repeated, a little disappointed.

"Do you know who lived here before you?" Mandie asked.

"Nobody. We built this here house ourselves," the man replied.

"But your sign says *Fine Food Since 1852*," Sallie objected. "That would be forty-eight years ago."

"Oh, that's because the other owners didn't have much of a house. The roof fell in when a heavy snow came one winter. They sold it to us and we built a new house," the man explained.

"And they owned a store and a restaurant, too?" Joe asked.

"This here is a boardinghouse, young fella, and a store," the man replied. "That's what they had, too, so we just kept their sign to put on our door."

"Do you know who the other people were?" Mandie asked.

"No, don't recollect who they was," the man said. "You see, it was my grandpa that bought it from them, and he handed it down to my pa, and he gave it to me, and they're all dead now."

"Do you remember anyone having the name Hezekiah, or ever hearing anyone mention the name?" Joe asked.

"Don't believe I do. Only thing I remember for sure was that these other owners had built their house on the site where an old house had burned down many years ago," the man told them.

"Has there ever been any other house near here?" Mandie asked.

"Not that I can remember," the man said. "Where you younguns from? Are you looking for long-lost relatives or something?"

Mandie and Joe looked at each other. It wouldn't do to let anyone know there was supposed to be buried treasure somewhere near here.

"I live in town with my Uncle John Shaw and my mother," Mandie replied. "We were just walking around and thought we'd see if we could find some old property of some of their friends from long ago."

"Oh, yes, I know John Shaw when I see him. Sorry I can't help you." He shook his head. "I've got to go in the back now and see how the cooking is coming along for supper," he said, starting to leave.

"That's all right, sir," Joe said. "But I don't believe I got your name."

The man stopped. "Name's Jud Jenkinson. Y'all come back."

The young people turned and went out the front door. Once outside, they stopped to talk in the yard.

"This has got to be Hezekiah's house, or where it used to be," Mandie said. "I just know it is."

"It probably is," Sallie agreed.

"I don't know." Joe looked skeptical.

"Well, y'all hurry and decide whose house it be, so's we kin go home. Must be time to eat," Liza said, cuddling Snowball in her arms.

"You're right, Liza. It must be nearing suppertime," Mandie said. "Do y'all think we have time to measure the other distances from here?" She pulled the map out of her pocket. "It says it's 936 feet to a rock pile, but that's in a different direction from the way we came."

"I think we'd better head home," Joe said. "If we're late for supper, your mother may not let us go out again tomorrow."

"Besides, that doctor friend of Abraham's was supposed to come back," Sallie reminded them.

Mandie gasped. "Oh, I forgot all about him! Let's hurry! He may be there by now."

" 'Bout time to hurry home, ain't it, Snowball?" Liza grumbled, holding the kitten tightly.

When they got back to the house, Jason Bond, the caretaker, was sitting on the front porch waiting for them. "Where in tarnation have y'all been?" he asked. "You tell me to let you know when that doctor comes back to Abraham's house, and then you go off and don't even let me know where you are. And everybody else is gone off, too."

"Mr. Jason, I'm sorry. Has the doctor been back to see Abraham?" Mandie asked.

"Yep. Been and gone," the caretaker told her.

"Gone? Oh, shucks!" Mandie cried.

"Well, we can't be in two places at one time," Joe said.

"And he might not know anything anyway," Sallie added.

"Has dat Jenny got supper cooked wid out me?" Liza asked.

"I believe so. Everything is waiting for Mr. and Mrs. Shaw and Uncle Ned to come back," Jason Bond replied.

"In dat case, I'll jes' go on in," Liza said. Opening the screen door, she took Snowball with her inside the house.

"Where has everybody gone?" Mandie asked.

"I don't rightly know, Missy. Said they'd be back in time for supper," the caretaker replied. "I reckon they'll be here any minute now."

Aunt Lou appeared in the doorway and stood listening to the conversation.

"Let's go ask Abraham if Dr. Plumbley has left town or if he's coming back," Mandie said.

"Yes, he might be back," Sallie said.

"Come on." Joe led the way down the front steps.

"Don't go nowhere now," Aunt Lou called to them as they hurried around the house. "Git in here and git washed up for suppuh."

Ignoring Aunt Lou, they found Abraham on the front porch again, rocking and drinking coffee.

"Here's your rope and your hoe," Joe said, laying them on the end of the porch.

"Done missed him," Abraham said as they walked up the steps.

"I know. Mr. Bond told us," Mandie said. "Is he coming back again?"

"Maybe tomorruh or de next day," Abraham replied. "He has to doctor his brother. He be good and sick."

"I'm glad Dr. Plumbley's coming back, but I'm sorry his brother is so sick," Mandie said.

"Tomorrow or the next day," Joe repeated. "You know what tomorrow and the next day are, don't you, Mandie? Tomorrow is Sunday and the next day is Monday. Sallie and I both have to leave on Monday to go back to school."

"Maybe he'll come back tomorrow," Mandie said.

"We need to spend the day tomorrow measuring off the other distances on the map to see if we can find anything else," Sallie said.

"Ain't y'all got nuthin' to do but go 'round measurin' things?" Abraham asked. "Y'all ain't even stayin' home long 'nuff to have comp'ny."

"Company?" Mandie asked. "We're not expecting any company. All our company has left except Uncle Ned, Joe, and Sallie."

"Dat lil' girl what live next do', she been over heah two time dis afternoon lookin' fo' y'all," the gardener said.

"You mean Polly?" Joe asked.

"Dat her," Abraham replied. "I heah her come over

two times and aks Aunt Lou where you at."

Mandie sighed. "Aunt Lou didn't know where we were. But, anyway, I guess Polly will come back later."

"I think we had better go get washed up before your mother gets home, Mandie," Sallie warned.

"Abraham, just in case your doctor friend happens to come back tonight unexpectedly, will you please come and let us know?" Mandie asked.

"He won't be back tonight. Too far," Abraham replied. "But I let you know when he do come back."

The young people went through the back door of the house. As they entered the long hallway inside, the kitchen door was open, and they could see Jenny stirring pots and moving about, getting the meal ready.

"Let's go through the kitchen," Mandie said, quickly entering the room.

"Something smells good!" Joe exclaimed. He tried to look into the pots on the big iron cookstove.

"Outta dem pots, boy!" Jenny scolded. "Ain't done yet nohow!"

"Oh, Jenny, can't I even look?" Joe teased.

"Nope," Jenny said, shaking a spoon at him. "Git!"

"All right, we'll git . . . Mrs. Davis," Mandie said slyly.

Jenny dropped the spoon she was holding and turned to look at Mandie. "You talkin' to me, Missy?" She picked up the spoon, took it to the sink, and rinsed it off.

"You are Mrs. Davis, aren't you?" Mandie replied.

Joe stood by, tightening his lips.

"What you talkin' 'bout, Missy? My name Jenny," the Negro woman said.

"I know. Your name is Jenny Davis," Mandie said. "Abraham told us."

"Who dis Abraham?" Jenny turned back to the stove.

"Jenny," Mandie chided, "we know Abraham, the gardener, is your husband. Why won't you go back and live with him? You do still love him, don't you?"

Jenny stood there, speechless.

"Mandie, I think we had better hurry and wash up," Sallie prodded.

"Yes, let's go," Joe said, walking toward the door.

Mandie stepped up close to Jenny. "Abraham still loves you," she whispered quickly.

Jenny's eyes filled with tears, and she dropped the spoon down into the big pot.

In the hallway Joe waited for Mandie. "You shouldn't go messing in other people's business, Mandie," he scolded.

Mandie smiled. "I'm not messing in anybody's business. I'm just trying to fix things up a little."

"I know about your kind of fixing up," Joe replied. He bounded up the stairs ahead of the girls to clean up.

"Do you think Abraham and Jenny will ever get back together again?" Sallie asked as they walked slowly to Mandie's room.

"If I can figure out how to finagle things around, they will." Mandie laughed. As she walked by the full-length mirror in the corner of the room, she shrieked. "Oh, I have to change dresses. I'm filthy!" she cried.

"So am I. We had better hurry," Sallie said.

They quickly washed up and changed clothes and were back downstairs shortly after Joe came down and the adults returned.

At the supper table the young people told the adults about their afternoon measuring.

"We found a house that I know must have been Hezekiah's," Mandie said.

"You mean it *may* be where Hezekiah's house *might* have been," Joe corrected her.

"Where is this?" Uncle John asked, looking up from the ham he was slicing.

"It's down on a main road about a mile from here," Mandie replied. "We traced an old dirt path by the cemetery down to this road, and there was the house. A man named Jud Jenkinson owns it, and he said he knows you, Uncle John."

"Jud Jenkinson? Yes, he owns a boardinghouse. Is that the house you're talking about?" Uncle John asked.

Mandie nodded, then proceeded to tell her uncle about the 1852 sign and the previous house.

Uncle Ned looked up. "House burn down," he said. "Old people die."

"You remember it, Uncle Ned?" Mandie asked excitedly. "Who were the people? Was one of them named Hezekiah?"

Uncle Ned shook his head. "No remember name," he said. "Old man, old woman. Die."

"Probably Hezekiah is dead. That is why we cannot find anyone who knew him," Sallie said.

"Does Mr. Jenkinson not know who lived there before his family, dear?" Elizabeth asked.

"No. He said his grandfather bought the place from the previous owners, and then his father owned it, and now he owns it. All the others are dead," Mandie said, biting into a hot buttered biscuit.

"What are you all planning to do next?" Uncle John asked, passing the sliced ham. "Are you going to keep on looking for clues on the map?"

"We thought we'd go back to that house and then measure off the 936 feet to the rock pile if we can find it.

And then on to the other places Ruby put on the map," Mandie replied.

"You know you will have to take someone with you again, Amanda, if you're going that far away," Elizabeth reminded her.

"Not Liza, please," Joe muttered under his breath.

"Tomorrow is Sunday, so we'll all go to church in the morning," Uncle John said. "Then after the noon meal, you young people can get back to your prospecting."

"On Sunday, John?" Elizabeth asked. "They should stay home and respect the Lord's Day."

"I don't think this once will hurt. They have to go back to school next week, and I do believe they have been exceptionally well-behaved lately," Uncle John said, winking at Mandie.

"Just this one time," Elizabeth conceded.

"Thank you," the young people said.

Mandie smiled at Uncle John. "Who is going with us?" she asked.

"We are having Mr. and Mrs. Turner over tomorrow afternoon, dear, so I suppose you'll have to take Liza with you again," Elizabeth told her.

"Liza!" Joe exclaimed.

"Well, I guess she'll do if nobody else can go." Mandie sighed.

"What do you mean by that, Amanda?" Uncle John asked.

"She's afraid of everything. Snowball found us somehow and nearly scared the daylights out of her," Mandie said, laughing.

Liza had stepped into the room and stood by the door, listening. She danced up to the table with a platter of hot biscuits. "Dat's right, Missy," she said. "Dat white kitten skeered me good. I ain't goin' no place like dat wilderness no mo'. No, I ain't!"

"Liza, Mother just said you'd go with us tomorrow so we can keep on with our search," Mandie told the girl.

Liza picked up the empty platter from the table and replaced it with the one of hot biscuits. She glared at Mandie. "I'd druther stay heah and hep Jenny cook."

"Liza, we have to have somebody go with us, and you're the only one not busy," Mandie said.

"Not busy? I stays busy all de time. I does," Liza insisted.

"If you would rather stay here and serve tea tomorrow afternoon for our guests, that will be all right, Liza. The Turners are coming," Elizabeth told her.

Liza's eyes grew wide. "De Turners? You say de Turners is comin'? No, ma'am. I go wid Missy," she said, quickly leaving the room.

Joe laughed. "What's wrong with the Turners?"

"The last time they were here, Liza accidentally spilled a cup of tea, and it splashed on Mrs. Turner's dress," Elizabeth explained with an amused look on her face. "Mrs. Turner naturally was quite upset, and she yelled at Liza. Now Liza is afraid of the woman."

"For our sakes, I'm glad she is," Mandie teased.

"So we will continue our search tomorrow after church, and Liza will go with us," Sallie summed it all up.

"Yes, and we're going to have to hurry. Time's running out," Joe warned.

Chapter 6 / The Old House on the Rock Pile

As soon as the young people could finish eating their noon meal after church services the next day, they took Liza with them and went to Abraham's house in the backyard. He was inside having his own meal, and they had to knock. Joe picked up the rope and the hoe still on the porch.

Abraham opened the door. "I'se eatin' my dinnuh now. What y'all wants?" he asked.

"We want to tell you we're going back down that dirt path behind the cemetery to measure some more. If your doctor friend comes while we're gone, would you please tell him we want to see him?" Mandie asked.

"Measurin' on Sunday? Dis de Lawd's day. Y'all s'posed to sit and read de good book," Abraham reproved them.

"We know that, Abraham, but Mr. and Mrs. Shaw made this one exception for today because we have to leave tomorrow to go back to school," Joe explained.

"Measurin'! Cain't find nuthin' else to do?" the old gardener grumbled. "I'll tell Samuel, but if he's in a hurry, he won't wait fo' you to come back."

"Thanks, Abraham," Mandie said. "We'll hurry."

"Git on yo' way. I'se got to finish my dinnuh," Abraham told them, closing the door.

"For goodness sakes, does Abraham never get in a good mood? He's always fussing," Joe mumbled.

"If you'd lost your wife a few days after you were married and you had to live alone when she lived right next door, you'd be fussy, too," Mandie remarked.

They headed out the front gate.

"I'd have better sense than to lose her in the first place," Joe said. "There's just no excuse for them to live apart."

"Maybe it's bettuh to live apart than to live together and fuss," Liza said, picking up Snowball who was following.

"Maybe, Liza, but how do we know they would fuss at each other if they lived together, anyway?" Mandie asked.

"I don't know about them, but when I marry you, Mandie, we are not going to ever fuss," Joe stated firmly.

"It is a long time until you grow up," Sallie said. "Everything may change by then. You may not want to marry each other. I do not think I would like to plan so far ahead."

Mandie blushed slightly.

"Right now we need to hurry and find this hidden treasure before we all have to go back to school," she reminded them.

The four of them hurried down the dirt path to its end at the main road.

"It didn't take long dis time, did it?" Liza said as they stood looking across the road at Mr. Jenkinson's boardinghouse.

"That's because we didn't have to worry about measuring and counting and digging out paths to get through," Mandie replied. She pulled the map out of her apron pocket and unfolded it.

"Y'all ain't plannin' on goin' into no mo' wilderness, are you?" the Negro girl asked.

"That depends," Joe replied, looking at the map over Mandie's shoulder. "You see we have to find a rock pile that is 936 feet from here."

"A rock pile? Lawsy mercy, what in dis world you want wid a rock pile?" Liza asked.

"We don't really want the rock pile, Liza. We just have to find it and then measure 572 feet from it to find a persimmon tree," Mandie explained.

" 'Simmon tree?" Liza questioned. "You ain't plannin' on eatin' no 'simmons, are you? Dey taste sumpin' awful."

Sallie smiled. "We know, Liza, but we are not going to eat any."

Joe looked at the map again. "And from the persimmon tree we have to measure 333 feet to a rhododendron bush," he said.

"Now what fo' y'all has to measure to find a 'dendrum bush when there's piles of 'em growin' in de yard at home?" Liza asked, puzzled.

"But this one is special," Mandie said. "There's something special about it that we have to find out."

"Special? Humph! I s'pose it blooms green or sumpin'."

Joe glanced up from the map, looking back the way they had come. "Do you see what I see?" he asked.

Everyone turned to look. Darting in and out of the bushes, Snowball bounced along, trying to catch up with them.

"Dat white kitten! Y'all went off and left it. De po' lil' thing done walked all dis way," Liza said. She ran to pick him up. "Come here, you po' lil' tired kitten. I'se gwine t' carry you de rest o' de way, I is."

Snowball curled up in Liza's arms and purred.

"I know I shut him up in the kitchen." Mandie sighed.

"That's not a good place to leave him. So many people go in and out of the kitchen, he's sure to get out," Joe said.

"He wants to go everywhere you do, Mandie," Sallie observed.

"I wish he had stayed home this time," Mandie said. "Liza, if you get tired of carrying Snowball, I'll take him. I don't think we'd better let him down. He may get lost."

"I carries dis po' lil' kitten. He be tired," Liza said. "Y'all jes' git on wid yo' measurin' rock piles and 'simmon trees and such. I'll take care o' Snowball."

"Thank you, Liza. I'm sure Snowball appreciates it," Mandie said.

Joe studied the map again. "If that's the place where Hezekiah's house used to be—across the road there— then according to the map, when we turn around, we should angle back to our right to find the rock pile," he concluded.

"But the path to Hezekiah's house on the map doesn't show a big road like this one. It must have been made since then," Mandie said.

"Even if the road was not there, the rock pile should be back in the direction Joe says," Sallie agreed.

"We do have to measure from that house though," Mandie said.

"And measure across the road backtracking to the right," Joe explained.

"The road is about fifty feet wide, and it's about fifty feet from the road to the house, so that's one hundred feet to here," Joe said, indicating the edge of the road.

"At least it's clear land for a while," Mandie said as the group surveyed the area ahead.

"So now we go 836 feet to the rock pile," Sallie said.

"Here we go," Joe said. He started off at an angle to their right. The girls helped stretch the rope between the three of them. Liza followed.

"Where we gwine now?" Liza asked.

"We're aiming right straight to those woods down yonder." Mandie pointed.

"Woods? I ain't gwine through no briary woods," Liza grumbled, holding Snowball closely.

"Remember, Liza, you have to go with us wherever we go. We can't leave you standing here, and my mother told you not to let us out of your sight," Mandie reminded her. "Of course if you'd rather go home and serve tea to the Turners—"

"I ain't gwine home," Liza interrupted. "I go wid you."

As Joe led the way, the girls counted aloud in unison. It was about five hundred feet to the woods, and there they had trouble.

"There are so many trees here, Joe, how can we measure in a straight line?" Mandie asked.

They all just stood there, staring at the thick woods in front of them.

"We'll just have to step around the trees and hope we figure right," Joe said.

"We only have about 336 feet more before we get to the rock pile," Mandie reminded them, "so maybe it won't take long to get through these trees."

"Chiggers! Dat's what y'all gwine to git," Liza muttered.

"We'll have to take that chance," Joe told the Negro girl. "Let's go."

Liza followed along, carefully holding her long skirts against her with one hand and clutching Snowball with the other.

When they finally came into a clearing, they stood there for a moment, looking around.

"It was 300 feet through the woods. That leaves about 36 feet to the rock pile," Mandie calculated. "We'll have to guess at 36 feet because the rope is one hundred feet long. 36 feet would be a tiny bit more than one-third of the rope."

"Does anybody see a rock pile?" Joe asked.

They all looked about. There was an old house across the clearing, but they couldn't see a rock pile.

"I wonder if anyone lives in that house over yonder," Sallie said.

"If someone does, I hope we're not on their property," Joe replied.

As they walked on, they kept looking for a rock pile, but there was nothing but dirt and weeds.

They were within fifty feet of the old house when Mandie suddenly stopped and pointed. "The house!" she exclaimed. "It's sitting on a rock pile!"

"Do you think this is the rock pile on the map?" Sallie asked as they walked around the house.

"It's the only one I can see anywhere," Joe said.

"I wonder why someone would build a house on a rock pile," Mandie said.

"Gotta have sumpin' fo' de house to sit on," Liza remarked. She held on to Snowball and followed the others.

"It is rock all the way around," Mandie noted as they came back to the front.

"We should knock on the door and see if anyone lives here," Sallie suggested.

"It looks empty, but I'll go see," Joe offered. As he put his foot on the first step to the front porch, a shot rang out above their heads.

A gruff voice yelled from inside the house. "That's fur 'nuff! Don't come no further! Whadda you want?"

Joe jumped backward.

Mandie reached to join hands with him and Liza as Joe grabbed Sallie's hand. Quickly, Mandie whispered, "What time I am afraid, I will put my trust in Thee."

They were all afraid to move. Their hearts pounded. Liza squeezed Snowball so hard he pushed his claws into her dress in fright.

The man inside the house yelled again. "I said whadda you want?"

"We're looking for a rock pile," Joe began.

"Rock pile?" the man yelled back.

The front door creaked noisily open. A dirty, bearded man stood there pointing a rifle at the young people. "What're you talkin' 'bout? A rock pile?" He looked from one to another. For some reason he singled out Liza in the group. "You there, what are y'all after?" he asked.

"Why, we's jes' after a rock pile, a 'simmon tree, and a ... a ... dendrum bush," Liza told him in a trembling voice. She tried to hide behind Mandie.

"What kind of dad-blame nonsense is that? I wanta know," he yelled.

"We were just measuring some distances and—"

"Measuring distances for what?" the old man interrupted, still pointing the rifle at them.

"We were just wondering how far it is from here to my house," Mandie spoke up.

"And where's your house at?" the man asked, spitting tobacco juice out into the yard near them.

Liza whispered in Mandie's ear. "Nasty, ain't he?"

Mandie jerked on her hand to shut her up. "My house is my Uncle John Shaw's house in Franklin right over that way," she told the man, waving her hand to the left.

"John Shaw, huh? He your uncle you say?"

"He was my father's brother," Mandie explained.

"I know all about them Shaws. What are you doin' this fur from home?" the man asked.

"We were just measuring to see how far we had come," Mandie replied.

"Well, you kin jest measure right off this here land. I'm stakin' a claim to it," the old man persisted, shaking his rifle at them. "John Shaw's got 'nuff. He ain't gittin' this here land."

"You mean nobody lives here?" Joe asked.

"Jes' me," the old man said. "Me and my rifle."

"Is your name Hezekiah by any chance?" Sallie spoke up.

"Who? Hezekiah? No, by granny's, it ain't Hezekiah," the man said.

"Did you ever know anyone living around here named Hezekiah?" Mandie asked.

"No, I ain't never knowed no Hezekiah. Now git off my land, all of you, 'fore you wish you had," the man warned.

"Yes, sir. We'll go," Joe said, turning to leave. Then he looked back. "You didn't tell us your name."

"My name ain't none of your bizness," the old man yelled.

"Do you know if there are any persimmon trees growing around here?" Mandie asked.

"Persimmon trees? What would I know about persimmon trees? But I'll tell you right now. Anything growin' 'round here belongs to me. Don't let me catch you puttin' your hands on it," the old man said. "Now are you goin', or you want me to force you off?"

"We're going," the young people all said at once. Hurrying away from the house, they ran on toward the woods, glancing over their shoulders to see if the man was following. Once inside the protection of the woods, they dropped to the ground, out of breath.

"Whew! That could have been dangerous." Joe gasped for air.

"Yes, that man is not just right, is he?" Sallie asked.

"He sure scared me," Mandie said.

"Dat man got lots of screws loose," Liza exclaimed.

Snowball left Liza's lap to crawl over to Mandie's.

Mandie took him in her arms and squeezed him. "Snowball, you'll have to stay with Liza a little longer," she said. Handing him to the Negro girl, she stood up.

Liza petted Snowball. "We ain't found no 'simmon tree yet," she complained.

"No, we still have to look for it. I'm afraid to go back toward that old man's house, so we'll have to estimate how far we've come," Mandie said.

"I'd guess we're about a hundred feet away," Joe calculated. "So if his house is where the rock pile is on the map, we should find a persimmon tree over that way about 472 feet," he said, pointing.

"We'd bettuh hurry up and git dis thing done, whatever we's doin'," Liza said. "I don't like all dese woods."

"Let's measure from here," Joe said. "It probably won't be exactly right, but I think we'll be pretty close."

When they had measured the 472 feet, they looked all around. There was not a single persimmon tree in sight. They walked around in circles, through trees and bushes and could not find even one.

"No persimmon tree of any kind anywhere?" Mandie moaned.

"We might not be in the right spot," Joe suggested.

"Persimmon trees do not live forever," Sallie reminded them. "The persimmon tree on the map might have died or been cut down."

"Dat's right. Somebody might not like 'simmons and dey jes' cut de tree down to git rid of it," Liza added.

"Should we look for the rhododendron bush?" Mandie asked. She looked at the map. "It says here the rhododendron bush is 333 feet from the persimmon tree."

"That's not so far. Maybe if we measured 333 feet in every direction from right about here, we could find the rhododendron bush," Joe suggested.

The others agreed, but after measuring 333 feet in several directions, they could not find a rhododendron bush. Then suddenly they found themselves in dozens of rhododendron bushes. Exasperated, they looked all around them.

"We only want one rhododendron bush!" Mandie exclaimed.

"But we have dozens of them," Sallie said.

"Take dat one over there. It looks like a good one. Want me to hep you dig it up?" Liza asked, pointing to a large bush.

"No thanks. You don't exactly understand what we're doing, and it's too hard to explain," Joe told the girl.

"I do not believe any of these rhododendron bushes

could be fifty years old," Sallie told them as she looked about.

"I have no idea how long they live, but you're probably right," Mandie agreed.

"Looks like we've lost out," Joe remarked.

"I'm not giving up," Mandie protested. "We'll find the hidden treasure somewhere."

"Hidden treasure?" Liza exclaimed. "Is dat what y'all been huntin' all dis time? Hidden treasure?"

Mandie and Joe exchanged glances.

"We're not sure what we're looking for," Joe told her.

"Whatever it be, it must be hid good," Liza said.

"Do you think we should go back to the house? Abraham's friend might be back by now," Sallie said.

Mandie sighed. "I hate to quit now. We don't have much time left."

"We can come back as soon as we check with Abraham," Joe suggested. "It's not all that far now that we've measured the distance and know the way."

"Reckon dem Turners done left by now?" Liza spoke up.

Everyone laughed.

"They probably have," Mandie assured her.

"Let's head back," Joe urged. He led the way, and Sallie followed right behind, but Mandie walked along by Liza.

As they made their way back down the dirt pathway, Liza pulled at Mandie's skirt. "Missy," she whispered, "sumpin' I fo'git to tell you."

Mandie frowned. "What is it, Liza?"

"Dat Missy Polly she done been back to yo' house dis mawnin' wantin' to know what y'all doin'. She wants to go wid you wherever."

"Why didn't you tell me then?" Mandie asked.

Liza smiled. "Oh, Missy, you know why I don't tell." She lowered her voice. "Dat Missy Polly she jes' wanta be 'round de doctuh son, dat's what she want. I tries hard to keep her 'way from de doctuh son fo' you."

Mandie laughed. Joe and Sallie turned to see what she was laughing at.

"What's going on back there?" Joe called back.

"Nothing really," Mandie replied. "Just something funny Liza told me."

As everyone trudged on, Liza bent to whisper to Mandie. "Ain't nuthin' funny. It serious."

Mandie smiled and said, "Thanks for telling me, Liza. I'll watch out."

Chapter 7 / Who Was Hezekiah?

As soon as they came within sight of the cemetery, Liza raced ahead. She didn't like being near that place. When the others came around the corner of the cemetery, they spied a horse and buggy standing at the hitching post in front of the house.

"Dr. Plumbley is at Abraham's!" Mandie exclaimed.

Joe and Sallie raced after her around the house to Abraham's little cottage. Liza, not knowing what it was all about, decided to follow. Holding on to Snowball, she caught up with them. Abraham and Dr. Plumbley were sitting and rocking on the front porch.

Mandie sat on the steps in front of the two men. "Dr. Plumbley . . ." she said, out of breath, "I'm so glad . . . we caught . . . you . . . before you left this time."

Dr. Plumbley smiled. "I believe you all have been running," he said.

They nodded, and Sallie joined Mandie on the steps. Joe put the rope and the hoe on the end of the porch and sat beside the girls.

Liza looked around. "Don't see no Turners nowhere," she muttered. "Must be gone. Snowball, we go see." She took the kitten and headed for the Shaws' house.

Mandie looked up at the big Negro doctor. "Dr. Plumbley," she began again, breathing a little easier, "Abraham said you used to live here in Franklin."

"Sure did, many years ago. I was born in Franklin and lived here with my grandparents until they died," the doctor replied. "I was twelve years old then, and I had to go to New York and live with relatives. My brother, Elijah, was luckier. Some friends here in Franklin took him into their home. He was only nine years old."

The young people looked at each other.

"What year did you leave Franklin?" Joe asked.

"I remember that very well. It was Easter Sunday, 1852, right after my grandparents' funeral. My aunt in New York had come down, and I went back with her that day," he said.

"What are y'all doin', takin' a census or sumpin'?" Abraham spoke up.

"No," Mandie replied. "We're trying to find people who lived here in Franklin in 1850. I want to show you something." She pulled the copy of the map out of her apron pocket and spread it on the floor by the steps. "Will you look at this, Dr. Plumbley?"

Abraham and the doctor got up and sat by Mandie on the steps.

Dr. Plumbley's face lit up as he read the map. "Where did you get this?" he asked.

"We found it in the attic tacked to the back of an old sideboard. Did you know my aunt, Ruby May Shaw, who drew this map?" Mandie held her breath, awaiting his answer.

Dr. Plumbley looked at her and smiled sadly. "Yes, I knew Ruby. She was like an angel on earth. She was so good and kind." He pulled out a handkerchief and dabbed the corner of his eye.

"You did!" Mandie exclaimed.

Sallie and Joe crowded closer.

Dr. Plumbley pointed to Hezekiah's house on the map. "That's where my grandparents' house was. I lived there."

"*You* lived there?" Sallie cried.

"Did you ever know anyone named Hezekiah?" Joe asked.

"I sure did. I knew him well. I am Hezekiah," Dr. Plumbley said.

All three young people bombarded him with questions.

"But Abraham said your name was Samuel," Mandie argued.

"My name is also Hezekiah—Samuel Hezekiah Plumbley. Everyone else called me Samuel, but Ruby found out my other name was Hezekiah and it fascinated her. She insisted on calling me Hezekiah."

Mandie reached for the doctor's big black hand and squeezed it. "Oh, Dr. Hezekiah, I'm so glad to meet you and to find out that you really knew my father's little sister!" she exclaimed.

"And I'm delighted to meet Ruby's niece," Dr. Plumbley replied, putting his other hand on top of hers.

"Do you know anything about this map?" Sallie asked the doctor.

"Were you with Ruby when she buried whatever this treasure is?" Joe asked.

"No, to everything. This is the first time I ever saw or heard of a map," Dr. Plumbley said.

"Was your house on the main road way down yonder?" Mandie questioned. "There's a sign there now saying *Fine Food Since 1852.*"

"Right on that spot," he said. "I haven't been to Franklin in a long, long time, but I rode down that way yesterday. That big road has been cut through since we lived there."

"Was your house the one that burned down?" Sallie asked.

Dr. Plumbley nodded. "Yes. My grandparents died in the fire," he said softly. "It was Good Friday, and I was at the church services. Grandma was sick, and Grandpa was too feeble to get her out when the roof caught fire. Nobody lived close by, and I wasn't there to help. If I had been, I might have been able to rescue both of them."

Everyone was silent, sharing the doctor's sadness.

Dr. Plumbley wiped his eyes. "They say the Lord knows best," he continued. "I was in His house of worship when it happened, and my brother was with me."

"Where were your parents?" Joe asked.

"My grandparents were the only parents I ever knew. My ma ran off with some man after I was born, and my pa didn't want me or my brother. He left us with my grandparents. Neither my ma nor my pa was ever heard of again," Dr. Plumbley explained.

"Dr. Plumbley, you don't know anything about the rest of this map, do you?" Mandie asked. "Do you know where the rock pile, persimmon tree, and rhododendron bush are?"

Dr. Plumbley inspected the map again. "No, I'm sorry. I don't know where those things could be," he said. "The house, though, I believe, is where Ruby's little girlfriend Patricia lived."

"Uncle Ned said he thought her friend lived there. He said her father worked for my grandfather," Mandie said.

"Yes, everybody called the man Scoot. I don't know what his given name was. They moved away right after your grandfather closed the mine," the doctor recalled.

"Did you know that my Uncle John has reopened the mine?" Mandie asked.

"You mean that?" Dr. Plumbley looked shocked. "When your grandpa closed it, he said it would never be opened again."

"I know," Mandie replied. "But we wanted to hunt for rubies, so Uncle John got it fixed up. And then there was this man who said he wanted to buy it."

"Buy it? But your grandpa closed it because some of your grandma's ancestors are buried there," the doctor told her.

"You are so right," Joe said. "If we could have met up with you before we got involved in that mine, things would have turned out better."

"Uncle Ned knew about the burial grounds, but he wouldn't tell anybody," Mandie explained. "He said the Cherokees have different customs from the white people. But then I'm part Cherokee myself," she said proudly.

"When you mentioned Uncle Ned, are you talking about the old Indian who lived with your grandparents at one time?" the doctor asked.

Mandie smiled. "I certainly am. In fact, Sallie is his granddaughter."

Dr. Plumbley reached for Sallie's hand and smiled at here. "I loved your grandfather when I was a youngster. He was always so kind to everybody, and he knew everything. All the children loved him."

Sallie nodded. "They still do. I think I have a wonderful grandfather."

"He's visiting the Shaws right now," Joe informed him.

"But we have to go home tomorrow," Sallie said. "I live with my grandparents over at Deep Creek. Did you also know my grandmother, Morning Star?"

"Of course," the doctor replied. "But she couldn't speak English at all, so we weren't well acquainted."

Mandie laughed. "She still can't speak much English, but she's trying real hard to learn."

"And you, young lady," Dr. Plumbley said to Mandie, "I understand you are Mr. Jim Shaw's daughter."

Mandie nodded.

"I left Franklin before your father was ever born, but I've kept in touch with friends here, and I know about him. In fact, your Uncle John was only about four years old when I left. Seems a hundred years ago, doesn't it, Abraham?"

"Now we ain't dat old, Samuel. I be sixty-one come December, and you be one year younger than me," Abraham replied. "You jes' looks 'round, and you be seein' lots o' older people. Why, we jes' middle-aged, me and you."

"You'll probably live to be a hundred, Abraham." Dr. Plumbley laughed.

Joe shuffled his feet impatiently. "Dr. Plumbley, do you have any idea what Ruby might have buried?" he asked, anxious to continue their search.

"No, sorry. I never heard about this map. You say you found it tacked on the back side of an old sideboard in the attic? That puzzles me because Ruby said she had a trunk in the attic where she locked away her secrets and treasures. She wore the key to the trunk on a ribbon around her neck."

"We did find it on the back of the sideboard—when Uncle John was moving some furniture out of the attic," Mandie said.

Joe's eyes grew wide. "Have y'all been through all the trunks in the attic?" he asked.

"Goodness, no." Mandie replied. "There are trunks on top of trunks up there."

"It would take a long time to go through all of them because the furniture would have to be moved around to get to some," Sallie explained.

"After all these years that trunk may have been thrown out," the doctor said.

"No, I wouldn't think so. Uncle John says that he can't remember anybody ever cleaning out the attic," Mandie answered. "We found a wardrobe stuffed full of dolls that belonged to Ruby and some old important papers that Uncle John didn't even know were there."

"Tell us about Ruby," Sallie said, looking up at the big Negro doctor.

"Ruby was a beautiful little girl, dark hair and eyes, and a big smile that absolutely lit up her face." Dr Plumbley told them. "She liked to wear ruby-colored clothes and ribbons in her hair because that was her name. I think she was named Ruby because her papa discovered rubies in the mine the day she was born. He thought the sun rose and set in her. He was so proud of her."

"Uncle Ned said he wouldn't ever mention her name again after she got killed," Mandie said, "and that he wouldn't allow anyone else to mention her name around him."

"That's right. It just broke his heart. Even though he had John, and then later Jim, he was never as attached to them as he was to Ruby," the doctor explained. "But then she was his firstborn, and she was also the only girl."

"Uncle Ned said my grandfather just grieved himself to death after Ruby was killed," Mandie recalled. "And then my grandmother died soon after my father was born."

"I knowed yo' pa, Missy," Abraham spoke up. "I lived right here when he was bawn, and I stayed right here while he growed up."

Again Joe seemed anxious to get back to the subject of Ruby's treasure. "Dr. Plumbley, we were down in the old newspaper building Friday, going through old newspapers," he said. "We found the story about Ruby's death in one of the papers. Do you remember who the Negro boy was who found her after her pony threw her?"

A deep sadness covered Dr. Plumbley's face. "That Negro boy was . . . me," he said slowly. "I was—"

"You were the one who found her?" Mandie interrupted.

Dr. Plumbley nodded. "I was going over to your grandpa's house to get some eggs. He kept a lot of chickens, and he gave my grandmother all the eggs she wanted. I went out of my way to go past the ruby mine because I always liked to look around there when I got the chance. I was walking along the path when I heard a great commotion ahead of me.

"Then I heard an animal whining. I ran and ran until I came to the bend in the path where it goes around that huge oak tree. There I found little Ruby." His voice broke. "She must have been thrown from her pony up against that big oak. It was a terrible sight. I've never got it over it."

"Wasn't she used to riding?" Mandie asked quietly. "Or was the pony a new one for her?"

"Ruby rode like a streak of fire from the time she could sit up straight on a pony." Dr. Plumbley smiled sadly. "Your grandpa always said she rode like a real Indian papoose. And she had had that pony a long time. It was a beautiful Shetland." He paused a moment. "After the accident your grandpa ordered the pony shot, but Uncle Ned arranged for one of the young Indians from his village to take the pony away. He told your grandpa it had been shot and buried."

Mandie looked quickly at Sallie. "That sounds like your grandfather—soft-hearted for animals. But I've never known him to cover up the truth like that."

"You do not understand," Sallie replied. "It would have been cruel to kill the pony. My grandfather forgave the poor animal. Besides, no one knew what caused the pony to throw her. It might not have been the pony's fault."

"I understand," Mandie agreed. "I would have done the same thing. Dr. Plumbley, was Ruby already dead when you found her?"

"I think so. It must have been instant death. The commotion I heard must have been the pony throwing her off. When I found her, her neck was broken." He wiped his eyes with his handkerchief. "Even though I'm supposed to be a big, strong man now that I'm a doctor, I still feel shivers go over me when I remember little Ruby lying there. I remember thinking, she's too good to remain on this earth. God wants her home with his other little angels."

"Abraham, you didn't know her, did you?" Joe asked.

"No, I was too young when I left here. When I come back later all dis done happened," the gardener replied. "I does know, though, old Mistuh Shaw he never smiled no mo'. He not innerested in nuthin' no mo'."

"I ran like crazy," Dr. Plumbley continued his recollections. "Old Mr. Shaw was the first one I found here in the yard, so he's the one I had to tell. He was carrying the eggs in from the barn, and when I told him what happened, he went wild. He threw those eggs everywhere and ran back the way I had come."

Everyone sat silent for a moment.

"How long are you going to be here?" Mandie asked hesitantly.

"I don't know," the doctor replied. "My brother is still sick, and I took a little vacation to come down here and doctor him. So I'll be around until he mends."

"What I really meant was how long are you going to be here at Abraham's house today?" Mandie asked.

"If he'll give me something to eat, I might stay for supper. That is ... if he asks me." Dr. Plumbley grinned at his friend.

"You knows I'll give you sumpin' to eat. I can cook jes' as good as any woman, jes' 'bout," Abraham said.

"Except for one, right, Abraham?" Mandie teased.

Abraham frowned. "What you talkin' 'bout, Missy?"

"The one you haven't talked to for forty years," Mandie replied.

Abraham got up from the steps, dusted off the seat of his pants, and sat down in a rocking chair. "I ain't been knowin' no woman forty years," he said.

"I know what she's talking about, Abraham," Dr. Plumbley said. "I think it's time you brought Jenny home."

"Who's Jenny?" the old man asked stubbornly.

"Just think how nice it would be to have a woman in the house," the doctor told him.

"Look who's talkin'. You didn't git married yo'self till 'bout three year ago, after you done got to be a old man," Abraham replied.

"Why, you just said a while ago that we aren't old,"

Dr. Plumbley teased. "You well know I couldn't get married when I was young. I had to work very hard to get an education so I could go to medical school. I didn't have time or money to support a wife and family."

Liza came across the yard to Abraham's front porch. "Miz 'Lizbeth she say fo' y'all to git yo'selves in de parlor," she told the young people.

"All right," Mandie replied. "What does she want? Do you know?" She stood up, folded the map, and put it in her apron pocket.

"She say de Turners dey done gone. You come home now," Liza repeated.

The young people exchanged glances.

"We weren't waiting for the Turners to leave, Liza. It was you who didn't want to see them," Mandie reminded her.

"Is anyone else there?" Joe asked.

"Nope. Jes' Miz 'Lizbeth, Mistuh John, and dat Injun man," Liza replied.

Mandie turned to the Negro doctor, who was now standing on the porch. "Could you come over to the house with us and meet my mother and Uncle John. You said you know Uncle Ned already."

The doctor looked at his friend. "Abraham, what time are you going to have dinner?"

"Whenever you come back," he answered.

"I won't be gone long," Dr. Plumbley promised.

Mandie led the way back to the house and into the parlor. Grasping Dr. Plumbley's big hand, she stepped forward. "Mother, Uncle John, this is Abraham's friend, Dr. Samuel *Hezekiah* Plumbley from New York," she announced. "Uncle Ned, you already know him from way back, remember?"

Uncle Ned stood, looked the doctor over, and put his hand on the big man's shoulder. "This young Samuel Plumbley?" the Indian asked as he studied the smiling black face.

"That's me," Dr. Plumbley said, putting an arm around the Indian's shoulders. "You don't know how glad I am to see you again."

"Friend of Ruby," Uncle Ned said, a little excited, which was unusual for him. He turned to John and Elizabeth. "Friend of Ruby," he repeated.

Uncle John stood and gripped the doctor's hand. "You were a friend of my little sister's?"

"Yes, sir, I knew Ruby," Dr. Plumbley replied.

Uncle John introduced Elizabeth.

"How do you do, Dr. Plumbley? Please sit down," she invited.

The young people sat and listened as the adults discussed the same things they had been talking about.

Uncle John was happy to find a friend of his sister's, and Uncle Ned was delighted to see the small boy, now grown big and tall, who had known his dear little papoose, Ruby.

Chapter 8 / The Secret Hiding Place

As soon as the excitement subsided, Mandie asked her mother if she and her friends could look in the attic for the trunk that belonged to Ruby.

"A trunk?" Elizabeth questioned.

"Dr. Plumbley told us Ruby had a special trunk she kept all her secrets and treasures in," Mandie explained. "And she wore the key around her neck."

"Are you giving up on the map search?" Uncle John asked.

"Oh, no, sir," Mandie replied. "But we're at a dead end right now. I thought we might find something in Ruby's trunk."

"Go ahead and look, dear—all of you. But don't waste the rest of the day up there, and do be careful moving things around. Some of that furniture is heavy," Elizabeth cautioned.

The young people raced upstairs. When they reached the attic, they again despaired at the sight of so many pieces of furniture, boxes, trunks, and other discards.

"Let's start with the easy ones," Mandie said. "The trunks near the door are easier to get to."

She led the way and the three of them began opening trunks and searching the contents. As they worked their way deeper into the attic, they found trunks packed with old clothes, books, shoes, papers, dishes, blankets, linens, and even baby clothes.

"Look!" Mandie exclaimed, picking up a piece of white cloth. "Somebody's baby diaper!" She held it up for the others to see. "It'd be fun to know whose it was, wouldn't it?"

"Yes, it would be, but it could also be embarrassing," Sallie said.

"It might have been your Uncle John's when he was a baby." Joe laughed. "I'd hate for somebody to find a diaper I used to wear."

"And here are some booties, and bonnets, and sweaters. They're all white, so I don't know whether they were for a girl or a boy," Mandie said.

"My mother told me that when she was a baby everything was always white, whether it was for a girl or a boy," Joe said.

Mandie was still poking into the trunk when she felt something metal deep down below the clothes. Pushing things aside, she withdrew a large framed portrait of a baby dressed in a long white dress, lying in the arms of a beautiful young woman. "I've found something wonderful!" she exclaimed. "Just wonderful!"

Sallie and Joe rushed to her side to see what it was.

"It's just a portrait of a baby and its mother," Joe said.

"But look at the face of the mother." Sallie pointed.

Joe's eyes grew wide. "That is the same lady that is in the portrait hanging in the library."

"It's my grandmother! It is!" Mandie cried. "I wonder which baby this is."

"Leave that trunk open, Mandie, and after we get through, we can take the picture downstairs and see if your uncle knows who the baby is," Sallie told her.

"I hope he does," Mandie said. Placing the portrait on top of the baby clothes, she left the trunk open and continued on to the next trunk. "Sallie, your grandfather would probably know better than Uncle John because he saw all of them when they were babies."

"Yes, he would," Sallie agreed.

Joe opened another trunk and found some old decaying clothes. "What good is all this old stuff up here?" he asked. "Why don't you throw it out?"

"I think it ought to be cleaned out up here, too. I'll ask Uncle John about it when we have time to do it one day," Mandie said, opening a trunk that was almost empty.

Sallie, in the far corner, bent over a large trunk. "I think I have found something," she called.

Mandie and Joe hurried to look. The trunk was full of a little girl's clothes, many of which were ruby colored.

Mandie gasped. "These are Ruby's clothes!" She reached to pull some of the garments out of the trunk and then suddenly withdrew her outstretched hands. "How can I go through those things?" She shivered. "It's all so sad. Ruby seems so real to me now." Mandie's blue eyes filled with tears.

Joe patted her softly on the shoulder. "Maybe we should forget the whole thing . . ."

"Oh, no," Mandie protested. "We have to see if there is anything here that will help us find the treasure. It's just so sad."

"Want me to look?" Joe offered.

Mandie nodded as she stared at the things in the trunk.

"I will help you, Joe," Sallie volunteered.

Joe carefully removed the first garment. It was a ruby-red riding outfit. He shook out the wrinkles and handed it to Sallie, who placed it carefully on a nearby table.

One after another, Joe removed the contents of the trunk. Sallie put them in a neat pile on the table. There was not a thing in the trunk but clothes.

"Don't you think there must be another trunk?" Joe asked. "A rich girl like Ruby would have had a lot more clothes than this, wouldn't she?"

Mandie nodded and her voice trembled as she spoke. "But you know, when people die, you usually give their clothes to the needy. There may not be any more."

"Let's keep looking," Joe said. He and Sallie replaced the garments in the trunk and continued on.

They found lots of old clothes but no more that could have belonged to a ten-year-old girl.

"Didn't they wear funny-looking clothes back in the old days?" Joe asked as they searched a trunk of long dresses with hoops and ostrich feathers.

"We think they're funny, but to them that was the latest style," Mandie said. "I suppose years from now people will look at our old clothes and laugh at them." She began to brighten a little. "I'd like to know what the clothes will look like then. I imagine the dresses will be shorter and not so full because everything shrinks with time. Things get smaller and thinner."

"I had never thought about that, but it is true," Sallie agreed.

"We'd better hurry. The day is going by fast," Joe reminded the girls.

They went through every trunk that they could find and finally plopped down on an old settee.

"There just aren't any more of Ruby's things here, at least not in a trunk," Joe said.

"What about something other than a trunk?" Mandie asked, looking around.

"It would take hours and hours to go through all the furniture up here," Sallie said.

"Maybe we could search the furniture near the trunk that has Ruby's clothes in it," Mandie suggested. "When people brought things up here, they would put the things together that they brought up at one time, wouldn't they?"

"You mean if they cleaned out one room downstairs and brought all the furniture up here, they would place it all together?" Joe asked.

"Yes, more or less, depending on how much room they needed for it," Mandie replied.

"Maybe," Joe said.

"But we moved the furniture all around up here when we selected pieces for the Burnses' house," Sallie reminded them.

"That's right. We also decided that the oldest furniture was in that corner over there—" Mandie pointed. "—Because it would have been the first put in here, remember? It's also the hardest to get to."

"I suppose we could look in all the furniture in that corner," Joe said. He made his way over to it, stepping over boxes and sliding over the tops of chests.

Mandie and Sallie joined him. They opened dressers, looked in wardrobes and boxes, and were almost finished when Uncle Ned appeared at the doorway. He stood there watching them.

"That furniture older than Ruby," he called across the attic to them. "Not Ruby's. Belong to her grandma, grandpa."

"My great-grandparents? My goodness, it must be old!" Mandie exclaimed.

"Old. Older than me," Uncle Ned replied. "Furniture of Ruby still in Ruby's room."

"Ruby's room?" Mandie asked. The three waded through furniture, boxes, and trunks to get to Uncle Ned.

"She still has a room?" Sallie asked.

"Ruby's room on second floor near Papoose's room," Uncle Ned replied.

"Let's go see it. Show us which room it is," Mandie said excitedly.

"This girl has been dead fifty years, and she still has a room?" Joe said, unbelieving.

Uncle Ned led the way down the stairs to the second floor. He passed Mandie's room, went on down the hallway to the end, and opened the door. "This Ruby's room," he said, waiting for the young people to enter.

The room did not look like it belonged to anybody. It had an empty feeling about it even though it was full of mahogany furniture. There were no personal articles sitting around and no personal pictures or decorations on the walls.

Mandie walked over to the huge wardrobe and flung open the doors. It was empty. Sallie opened drawers in a chest of drawers. They were empty. Joe checked the dresser. It was empty, too.

The young people looked at each other and then at Uncle Ned.

"When Ruby die, Talitha take everything out of this room except furniture. She give it all away. Shut door, never use room," Uncle Ned explained.

"My Grandmother Talitha did that? Then she took everything out before Uncle John was old enough to remember," Mandie reasoned. "And he would have no memories of this room. He may have thought it was just another guest room."

"Is there anything at all in any of the drawers or anywhere?" Joe asked.

"No, not in drawers, not in furniture," Uncle Ned told them. "Ruby had secret hiding place. Talitha never found."

"Do you know where it is?" Mandie asked.

"I not like to bother. Just way Ruby left it," the old Indian said.

"My grandfather, you must tell us what you know," Sallie pleaded.

"How do you know about it when her mother didn't even know?" Joe asked.

"Ruby tell me secrets," Uncle Ned said sadly. "She show me secret place."

"And when she died, you didn't tell her parents about the secret place?" Mandie asked.

"Ruby tell me secret. I never tell secret," Uncle Ned replied. "Secret not to be told."

"My grandfather, please tell us," Sallie begged. "Ruby is long dead."

"Please," Mandie said. "We won't tell anyone else if you don't want us to."

"The secret place may have something in it about the treasure map," Joe suggested. "Do you know what's in it?"

Uncle Ned shook his head. "No, I never bother," he repeated.

"Is it in this room?" Mandie persisted.

"Are we near it?" Sallie asked.

Joe scratched his head. "Is it in the secret tunnel in this house?"

Uncle Ned hesitated for several moments then walked over to the tall fireplace with a huge mantlepiece. The fireplace was ornate and made in sections of marble with fancy brass strips running between and around the edges. He paused for a moment, and a sad expression flitted across his old wrinkled face.

Taking a deep breath, Uncle Ned reached up to the marble section on the left end. Carefully tugging away at the heavy marble, he managed to lift it up, disclosing a hollow space beneath it in the mantlepiece.

The young people hovered near, watching and waiting. They were all too short to see inside the space.

Joe reached for the tall footstool by the high, four-poster bed, and brought it over to the mantlepiece. Mandie stepped up on it and still had to tiptoe to see inside the section of marble.

"Uncle Ned, can I take things out so we can see what it is?" Mandie asked.

Uncle Ned nodded. "Can look but must put back."

Mandie carefully took a large white feather out of the opening and held it up for the others to see. "I wonder where this came from?" she asked. "It must be something special."

"Special school play. Ruby Indian in play," Uncle Ned informed them.

"She *was* half Indian," Joe remarked.

Mandie gave the feather to Sallie to hold, then turned back to the secret hiding place. A moment later she withdrew a thick cloth drawstring bag from inside. "Look!" she cried. Quickly untying the string, she stretched the top open and took out an exquisite necklace made of rubies. "Oh, look! This must be worth a fortune!" she exclaimed, dangling the necklace for the others to see.

"Yes, father of Ruby give to her when Ruby born. Belong to his mother," the Indian explained. "Was Ruby's most treasured thing."

"This was my great-grandmother's!" Mandie said, examining the necklace in awe. "We should tell Uncle John about this."

"Tell me about what?"

Everyone turned to see Uncle John standing in the open doorway.

"I was looking for y'all and heard you talking in here," he said.

Uncle Ned sighed. "Ruby have secret treasure place." He pointed to the opening in the mantlepiece.

Uncle John walked over to where Mandie stood on the footstool. "Why, the mantlepiece opens up. Did you know about this, Uncle Ned?"

"Yes, Ruby show me. This Ruby room. Promise never tell about place, but now Ruby gone," he said sadly.

"This was Ruby's room? I never knew," Uncle John said.

Mandie handed him the ruby necklace. "Uncle Ned told us that your father gave this necklace to Ruby when she was born. It was his mother's, your grandmother's."

"My grandmother's?" Uncle John turned the necklace over in his hands. "This is beautiful! And it has been here ever since Ruby died?"

"Yes," Uncle Ned answered. "I never bother. I not know what in hiding place."

Mandie reached into the hole again and pulled some papers from the opening. They were drawings Ruby had made of the house, animals, and unrecognizable people.

The last thing Mandie found was a tiny locket on a long gold chain.

"A locket!" Mandie gasped. She quickly stuck her fingernail in the catch. As the locket came open, cameo pictures of a man on one side and a woman on the other appeared.

"Uncle John!" Mandie quickly held out the locket to him. "Your mother and father?"

John looked closely at the pictures. "Yes, it is, Amanda."

"Oh, Uncle John," Mandie said excitedly. "Could I wear the locket sometime when I'm all dressed up for something special?"

"We'll see," Uncle John said. "I think all of these things are special, but the necklace and the locket especially need to go in my safe."

"You right, John Shaw," Uncle Ned said sadly. "Ruby not ever coming back."

"You kept your promise to her, Uncle Ned. And I think she would be glad you showed us the hiding place. These things are too precious to leave in a place like that." Uncle John put his arm around the old Indian's shoulders.

Uncle Ned looked down at the floor and Mandie detected tears in his eyes. *Uncle Ned never cries,* she thought. *He must have loved Ruby a lot.*

She jumped down from the footstool and took his wrinkled hand. "Uncle Ned, Ruby is not ever coming back, but I am here. I'm still your Papoose, remember?"

Uncle Ned squeezed her hand. "Yes, you always my Papoose. Remember, I promise Jim Shaw I watch over Papoose after he go to happy hunting ground," he said in a shaky voice. "So many already gone to happy hunting ground."

"Maybe I'll be around for a while, Uncle Ned. I'm only twelve years old, you know." Mandie smiled up at him.

Sallie gave her grandfather a hug. "I am not quite one year older than Mandie," she said. "And I hope to grow up, and get married, and have many little papooses for my grandfather to love."

Uncle Ned returned her hug.

"Well, it seems I got left out of all this," Joe teased. "I think we'd better be going, though, or the day will be gone."

"Let's go back up to the attic," Mandie suggested. "Uncle John, come with us. I have something I want to ask you about."

"Yes, go to attic," Uncle Ned said quickly. "More things belong to Ruby in wardrobe with dolls. Come," he said, leading the way to the attic. Taking them directly to the huge wardrobe, he indicated the big drawer at the bottom.

"That's the drawer where we found the map, remember?" Mandie said.

Joe pulled the drawer out.

"It looks like a lot of papers to me," Uncle John said.

"Under papers," Uncle Ned directed them. "Under papers."

The young people quickly began removing papers and envelopes and finally came to a small Bible at the bottom.

When Mandie picked it up and opened it, a paper fell out. "Why, it's a copy of the treasure map," she said.

"And the Bible belonged to Ruby, didn't it?" John asked.

The old Indian nodded.

Mandie turned the map over and read out loud a

handwritten note on the back, " 'Had to tack the other copy of my map behind the sideboard for the time being because I lost the key to my trunk. I must remember that the rhododendron bush is the one growing near the huge rock.' "

"More clues," Joe said.

"What else is in the drawer?" Sallie asked.

Mandie sorted through various cards and letters addressed to Ruby, several school books, pencils, hair ribbons. "Uncle Ned, how did you know about all this?" she asked.

"I put there. All I could save. Father of Ruby not want to see anything belong to her. I hide all this," he replied.

"Let's take that copy of the map back downstairs and show it to Dr. Plumbley," Joe suggested. "That is, if he's still here."

"He's still here," Uncle John said. "I came up to find y'all to say good-bye to him."

"Come on," Mandie urged, taking the map with her as she led the way downstairs. "Maybe he can help us figure out this note."

"I hope so, but I doubt it," Joe said.

"Yes, things have changed so much since then," Sallie added.

Uncle Ned followed last with a bowed head and stooped shoulders. "Samuel Plumbley know much," he muttered to himself.

Chapter 9 / More Clues

Halfway down the attic steps Mandie stopped. Uncle John was right behind her. "I forgot to show you something, Uncle John," she said. "Let's go back for just a minute. Uncle Ned, you, too. Joe and Sallie, you know what it is. We'll catch up with you downstairs in a minute."

"Don't take too long," Joe told her as he and Sallie went on down.

Mandie took Uncle John and Uncle Ned straight to the trunk where she had found the baby clothes. She picked up the portrait and held it up for them to see. "Look what I found in this trunk. It must be your mother, Uncle John, and either you, or my father, or Ruby as a baby," she said.

"I've never seen that before," Uncle John said. "But yes, that's definitely my mother."

"Uncle Ned, do you know which baby it is?" Mandie asked.

The old Indian moved closer to look. "That is Ruby. I here when man paint picture. These baby clothes belong to Ruby. Talitha save. Hope she have other little girl to wear clothes. But only boys, Jim and John."

"Why did she put this portrait in the trunk? Why isn't it hanging somewhere?" Uncle John asked.

"Father want everything of Ruby taken away—everything. I take things, hide in wardrobe. Talitha hide clothes here—this and other trunk. Everything else give away," Uncle Ned replied.

Uncle John put his arm around Mandie as he held the portrait on top of the baby clothes. "Where shall we hang this?"

"In the library," Mandie said quickly, "where my grandmother's portrait is."

"I'm not sure we can find enough wall space in the library to hang this there," Uncle John said.

"All we have to do is move my grandmother's portrait to one end of the fireplace and hang this one at the other end," Mandie suggested. "I believe they're the same size."

"Now why didn't I think of that?" Uncle John asked. "We'll do that before you go back to school. Let's just leave it here for now. I imagine Dr. Plumbley is getting impatient with us by now. He was getting ready to leave."

"Oh, no!" Mandie exclaimed as she rushed ahead of them down the stairs. She still had the copy of the map in her hand that they had found in Ruby's Bible.

In the parlor Joe and Sallie were trying their best to keep Dr. Plumbley talking so he wouldn't leave until Mandie got there. Elizabeth watched in amusement nearby.

"Here's Mandie now with the other copy of the map, Dr. Plumbley," Joe said as Mandie came through the doorway.

Uncle John and Uncle Ned followed her into the room and sat down near Elizabeth.

"I have it," Mandie said, waving the paper in the air as she hurried forward to sit on a chair near the doctor.

"Read the note on the back, Dr. Plumbley. Do you have any idea where this huge rock is that she said is near the rhododendron bush?"

Dr. Plumbley examined the paper, then handed it back to Mandie. "There are lots of rocks around this neck of the woods. And there are quite a few that a ten-year-old child would call huge."

"Do you remember any special rock that Ruby knew about?" Joe asked.

"Maybe one that was a little different?" Sallie added.

Dr. Plumbley thought for a minute and then shook his head. "No, I'm sorry. I can't remember any special rock offhand," he said, "and I'm afraid I'm going to have to be leaving." He stood.

All the young people jumped up.

"Dr. Plumbley, please go with us to look for this rock," Mandie begged.

"You know the area better than we do," Joe said.

"And you lived not far from the buried treasure, according to Ruby's map," Sallie said.

Dr. Plumbley laughed and looked at the adults, who were watching him. "What am I going to do with these young people? There are three against one," he said, shaking his head.

Uncle John laughed. "I'd say you'll have to give in to their wishes, or you'll never have another day's peace until you return to New York," he said.

"They can be persistent," Dr. Plumbley admitted.

"Sallie and Joe have to go back to school tomorrow, and I have to go Wednesday. We don't have much time. Please help us," Mandie pleaded.

"With you helping we could find this thing in no time, whatever it is," Joe said.

Dr. Plumbley looked from one to another of the young people. "Just what is it you want me to do?" he asked.

"Go with us to the place where your house used to be, and help us find the rock pile, persimmon tree, and rhododendron bush that are on the map," Mandie answered. "They're all near where you lived."

"And if I don't go?" the doctor asked.

"We won't get another holiday until Christmas. We'll have to wait until then to finish searching," Joe said.

"But that buried treasure has been in that spot for fifty years. It will stay there a little while longer, I'm sure," the doctor said, smiling.

"We do not know that it has been there for fifty years. Someone else may have already found it. We will not know until we find the place on the map," Sallie said.

"Why, even the spot may be gone," Dr. Plumbley reasoned. "Things may be so changed we'll never find it."

"Then you'll go with us?" Mandie asked.

Dr. Plumbley threw up his hands and laughed. "I surrender," he said. "Lead the way."

"Thank you!" Mandie grinned.

Joe and Sallie echoed her gratitude.

"Amanda, don't y'all be gone too long," Elizabeth said, as the group started to leave the room.

"We'll be back soon, Mother," Mandie replied.

"Wish us luck," Joe said, laughing.

"I hope you find whatever it is," Uncle John called to them.

As they went out the parlor door, Dr. Plumbley spoke to Mandie. "I must tell my friend that I'll be back soon. Remember, he's cooking supper for me."

"And we need to get his hoe and rope again," Joe said.

"The quickest way is through the kitchen," Mandie said, leading the way down the hall. "Come on."

As they entered the kitchen, Jenny stood at the table peeling potatoes. She looked up.

Mandie walked over to her and introduced Jenny to Dr. Plumbley as Abraham's wife.

Dr. Plumbley extended his hand. Jenny ignored the gesture and rushed over to the sink. "Y'all be on yo' way. I'se got a meal to cook."

"It was nice meeting you, Jenny. I hope I see you again sometime," Dr. Plumbley said.

Mandie quickly headed out the back door. "I don't think she was very nice to meet," she whispered to Sallie.

When they were all outside, Snowball came running to Mandie in the yard. She picked him up and carried him with her to the gardener's house.

Abraham sat on the front porch, rocking. " 'Bout time you come back, Samuel," Abraham fussed.

"I'm not back yet. You see, these nice young people have asked me to go on a treasure hunt with them. I just wanted to let you know I'll be back soon," Dr. Plumbley replied.

"Well, if you *ain't* back soon, I'll eat without you," Abraham warned.

Joe picked up the hoe and the rope from the end of the porch. "May we borrow these again, Abraham?" he asked.

Abraham nodded his head but said nothing.

"Do you want to go with us?" Mandie invited.

"I ain't gwine nowhere. And if y'all agwine, well, git!" Abraham snapped.

"Oh, you're grouchy just like Jenny," Mandie teased, petting Snowball in her arms.

"Dat Jenny ain't got nuthin' to do wid me, grouchy or not. Now git!" He rose and opened the front screen door. "And hurry back, Samuel, if you wants any supper."

"I sure do want some supper, so I'll be back soon," the doctor promised.

Using the hoe like a walking stick, Joe led the way across the road past the cemetery to the dirt pathway.

"I've been down this pathway many a time," Dr. Plumbley remarked, looking around as they walked along. "But, my, how things have changed! This path used to be much bigger, wide enough for buggies and wagons to go down it. And now it has just about disappeared under all these weeds and bushes."

"Wait till you see what we have to go through," Mandie warned.

"Joe had to chop out a pathway where it had all grown up," Sallie said.

When they came to that particular place, Dr. Plumbley couldn't believe all the trees growing there.

"This was wide open cow pasture when I left here forty-eight years ago," Dr. Plumbley said. "Guess I am getting old, no matter what Abraham says."

"I hope things haven't changed so much that you can't recognize these other places on the map," Mandie said.

"We'll see," the doctor answered.

When they came to the end of the path, they stopped to look across the road at the house with the sign *Fine Food Since 1852*.

"My grandparents' house was right where that big fine house sits now. It was only an old four-room house, two rooms downstairs and two upstairs. They were upstairs when the fire happened," Dr. Plumbley said softly, staring at the boardinghouse. "If they'd been downstairs, someone might have been able to save them. But the roof caught fire and that house went up like a bunch of kindling. If they could have only lived until I was grown and educated, I could have done so much for them."

Mandie took the doctor's big hand in hers. "But Dr. Plumbley, you probably wouldn't have gone to New York and become a doctor, would you?"

"Maybe. You see I lived with my aunt in New York. Her husband died, leaving her with some money they had saved. She wanted me to have it to use toward my education. I did repay her, though. I insisted on that."

"Well, what do we do now?" Joe asked.

"If you don't mind, I'd like to go over there and look around," Dr. Plumbley said.

"Come on. We've been inside and met Mr. Jud Jenkinson, the man who owns it now," Mandie said.

"Not inside. I'd just like to look around the yard," the doctor said.

They crossed the road and followed Dr. Plumbley around the house to the back yard. He stood there, looking about. The young people silently watched and waited.

"There it is!" the doctor exclaimed, pointing downhill and walking ahead. "It's still here."

They followed as he came to stop by a straggly old apple tree.

The doctor reached to touch the limbs. "The frost has already got the leaves, but this is the apple tree I remember," he said. "I used to swipe the apples and take them down there to eat." He pointed downhill to a small creek. "My grandmother always wanted to save them for pies and applesauce. And if she caught me, it was too bad. I wouldn't be able to sit down for a week." He laughed.

The young people smiled at each other.

"What did she whip you with that hurt so bad?" Mandie asked.

"She didn't do it. She'd get my grandpa to take his old leather razor strop and just about wear it out on me," the doctor said. "It sure hurt, but she knew what she was doing. She was teaching me to distinguish right from wrong. She was a good woman."

"Was your house in exactly the same spot as this one?" Joe asked.

"As far as I can tell, according to the well over there, our house was sitting directly behind this one," he said. "But then this big road has been cut through here, so it's hard to tell for sure. Things don't look the same."

"If *this* road wasn't here, what kind of a road did you have then?" Mandie asked.

"Just the dirt path we came down from the cemetery. It curved past our house and dead-ended into the creek down there," the doctor said. "This new road cut into part of it."

Mandie perched Snowball on her shoulder and held up the copy of the map. "You see, according to this, we have to count 936 feet to a rock pile. It looks like it goes back that way at an angle." She pointed.

Dr. Plumbley looked at the map and then at the direction Mandie was pointing. "That could be an awfully wide area," he said.

"We went that way and found an old house built on top of a rock pile," Joe said.

"And a terrible man camping out in it with a rifle," Sallie added.

"A man with a rifle?" the doctor asked, alarmed.

"We can stay far enough away from it so the man won't see us," Joe said.

"Well, let's hope he doesn't see us," Dr. Plumbley said. "Are you using that rope to measure off the distances?"

"Yes," Mandie replied.

"Then let's get started," Dr. Plumbley urged. "Here, let me take one end."

Soon they came within sight of the old house. Pointing through a small opening in the trees, Joe said, "That's the house over there on the rock pile."

Dr. Plumbley looked where Joe was pointing. "I don't remember that place being there. It might have been, but I don't remember it."

"Then maybe it *is* sitting on the rock pile that Ruby put on the map," Mandie said.

"It could be," the doctor agreed.

"If you think it is, then we should measure 572 feet and find a persimmon tree," Mandie reasoned.

"Only we looked for a persimmon tree and could not find a single one," Sallie said.

"Trees do die sometimes, and people do cut them down, you know," Dr. Plumbley reminded them.

"Well, anyway, let's measure it again and see if we can find one," Joe suggested.

At the end of the 572 feet the young people looked around.

"This isn't the same place we came to when we measured the distance this afternoon!" Mandie exclaimed.

"No, it is not," Sallie said.

Joe shook his head. "I still don't see any persimmon trees."

"Nor do I," Dr. Plumbley said.

"Do you recognize anything around here?" Mandie asked him. Taking Snowball in her arms again, she stroked his soft white fur absent-mindedly.

"Nothing looks familiar," the doctor answered.

"We must keep searching," Sallie said, looking around.

"Yes, we may be off the line of the map a little, but we can look close by for a persimmon tree," Joe agreed.

"We should mark the spot we measured to, so we will not lose it," Sallie said. She picked up a fallen limb. "I will put this right here."

After circling the area and still not finding one, they returned to the spot Sallie had marked.

"There could have been a persimmon tree around here back then," Dr. Plumbley told the disappointed young people. "I remember there were many of them between our house and Ruby's. But I haven't seen a single one today."

"Why don't we pretend this spot is a persimmon tree and measure 333 feet to find the rhododendron bush on the map?" Mandie asked.

"It may not come out right, but we can try it," Sallie agreed.

"Well, whatever we're going to do, let's hurry. I'm getting hungry," Joe said. "Which way do we measure?"

"That way," Mandie pointed at an angle to their left.

They came out into the same mass of rhododendron bushes they had found that afternoon.

"We've been here before," Joe said.

"I remember," Mandie agreed. "The map we just found in Ruby's Bible says the rhododendron bush is the one growing near the big rock."

"I don't see any rock. All I see is rhododendron bushes," Joe said.

Dr. Plumbley looked around. "Well, suppose we look

in between all these bushes and see if we can find a rock. How about that?"

"Good idea," Mandie said.

"That's gonna take forever," Joe moaned.

"Not quite that long, Joe," Sallie teased.

They thoroughly searched beneath and around all the bushes but found nothing. Snowball struggled to get down, but Mandie held him tightly.

As they came out on the far side of the bushes, Dr. Plumbley straightened up and looked around. "Wait a minute," he said, hurrying ahead. "I believe I recognize something!"

The young people quickly followed, and they soon came out of the bushes into a clearing. There, just ahead of them, was a huge boulder.

"The rock!" Mandie cried.

They all ran to look.

"I remember this rock very well now," the doctor said. "Ruby used to bring food for my grandparents, and she would meet me at this rock. How could I have forgotten?"

"Why did she bring it here?" Mandie asked. "Why didn't she take it to your house?"

"The Shaws' cook always came with her, but they were not allowed to go to our house because my grandma had tuberculosis, and they were afraid of catching it," he explained. "We had a schedule worked out between us. I would meet Ruby and the cook here at certain times."

"Did her parents know about this?" Joe asked.

"Oh, yes. They knew. They were very kind to us and were always doing things for us. They were good people," the doctor said.

"If this is the special rock on the map, all we have to

do is find the rhododendron bush that is the nearest to it," Mandie said.

They looked around and moaned. There were dozens of rhododendron bushes around the rock, any one of which could have been considered the nearest to the rock.

Joe sighed. "What are we going to do now?"

"That's a good question," Dr. Plumbley said, scratching his head.

Chapter 10 / The Map's Treasure

"We could dig all these bushes up and look under them," Joe suggested as they surveyed the mass of rhododendron bushes.

"My goodness, Joe, there're too many. We'd never get done," Mandie said, slowing petting her white kitten.

"We could narrow it down some," Dr. Plumbley remarked. "The small bushes must have grown up since Ruby buried her treasure."

"Would a rhododendron bush grow for fifty years?" Sallie asked. "If it was not cared for like these out here, would it not eventually die?"

Mandie and Joe shrugged.

"Sorry, I have no idea how long a rhododendron bush can live unattended," Dr. Plumbley said.

"If one did grow that long, wouldn't it be a good-sized tree by now?" Mandie asked.

"I never heard of rhododendron trees," Joe said.

Mandie looked at the map they found in Ruby's Bible. She pointed to the writing on it. "I think there is a mistake somewhere," she said. "The other map definitely said dig *three feet* under a rhododendron bush, and this map says dig *one foot*."

The others gathered around to look.

"In that case it won't take long to dig up the dirt around a few of these bushes and see if we hit something," Joe said. "One foot is not all that deep."

"But the soil washes," Sallie reminded them. "It has either washed more dirt over the place or washed dirt away from it. The land is sloped here, so I would say it washed the dirt away from it."

"You have great powers of deduction, Sallie," Dr. Plumbley said.

"She sure does," Joe agreed.

"I learn things from my grandfather," Sallie said.

"And her grandfather is the smartest man I ever knew," Mandie added.

"Since we only have one hoe, I'll start digging first," Joe volunteered. Taking the tool from Dr. Plumbley, he began walking around. "Let me find a place to begin."

Snowball again tried to wriggle free, and Mandie finally set him down.

"How about digging right here?" She indicated a place near the rock.

"All right. Here goes," Joe said, stomping the hoe into the ground.

The others stood around and watched as Joe loosened the soil among the bushes.

"Maybe we should go behind you and replant the bushes," Dr. Plumbley suggested.

"Yes, we should," Mandie agreed. "It would be a shame to dig up all these things and leave them to die."

"That's fine," Joe said, "but for goodness sakes, keep that cat away from me or he could get hurt."

Mandie bent down to call to her kitten. "Here, Snowball. Come here."

The white kitten stood there, looking at her. Then he took a flying leap into the rhododendron bushes and disappeared. Mandie and Sallie chased after him.

"Here, kitty, kitty!" Sallie called.

"Snowball! Come here!" Mandie searched underneath the bushes.

"Here he is," Joe yelled at them. Reaching down, he grabbed Snowball from under the bush he was digging up.

Mandie took her kitten and sat down on the grass nearby to hold him out of the way. Sallie joined her, and Dr. Plumbley stood, watching Joe dig.

Since Joe wasn't having any success, Dr. Plumbley finally spoke up. "How about letting me have that hoe a while, so you can rest?" he offered.

"Thanks," Joe said, handing him the tool. "All this may be for nothing. I'll start replanting the bushes."

Mandie turned to Sallie. "Would you hold Snowball for me so I can help Joe?" she asked.

"You just hold Snowball, and I will help Joe," Sallie said, getting up.

"I want to help, too, so you do a little and then hold Snowball while I do some," Mandie told her friend.

"All right," Sallie agreed.

Together she and Joe put the bushes back into the holes they had come out of and pushed the dirt up around them. Since Dr. Plumbley was using the hoe, they had to do the grimy work by hand.

Dr. Plumbley kept right on digging up bushes while they followed behind and replanted them. The doctor was bigger and stronger than Joe, so he was able to go faster.

"Let me help now, Sallie," Mandie said, getting up.

"I'm sorry my hands are so dirty for holding Snowball," Sallie said, brushing the dirt off her red skirt. She took the white kitten and sat down.

"That's all right. He'll wash himself if you hold him loose enough," Mandie said.

Sallie allowed the kitten to move about in her lap and wash his fur.

Suddenly Mandie stopped working and looked up. "Joe! I just thought of something! Whose land are we digging up? They might not like what we're doing," she exclaimed.

Joe continued with his work. "I don't know whose land this is," he answered.

Dr. Plumbley stopped digging and looked at her. "When I lived here, all this land belonged to your grandpa, Missy," he said.

"This far from the house?" Mandie asked.

"This is not really that far from your house. Your grandpa owned hundreds and hundreds of acres of land around here," the doctor said. "And he farmed most of it. There was some pastureland, but he had tenant farmers tending the land."

"Surely Ruby would bury her treasure only on their own property," Sallie reasoned.

"But I wonder if it still belongs to our family," Mandie said.

"If it does, why doesn't Mr. Shaw farm it?" Joe asked.

"Franklin has become quite a little city since I left here forty-eight years ago," Dr. Plumbley observed. "There's not as much farming being done. There are a lot of businesses here now."

"Your uncle is so rich that he probably does not need to grow crops," Sallie said to Mandie.

"He could grow crops and give them away if he

doesn't need anything," Mandie said with a sigh. "I suppose there are a lot of decisions to make and problems to solve when you get rich."

Dr. Plumbley continued to dig. "I wouldn't know about that," he said, laughing. "I've never been rich. I have enough income from my practice now to live on, but I'll never be rich."

"Yes, Mandie," Joe teased, "you're the only rich one here."

"I'm not rich, Joe Woodard," Mandie objected. "My uncle might be, but I'm not. I don't want to be rich," she said emphatically.

"I would like to be rich so I could help other people," Sallie said.

"I would like to be rich so I wouldn't have to work anymore," Joe said.

"You don't work, Joe. You go to school," Mandie argued.

"When I grow up I'll have to work," Joe told her. He stood a bush in its original hole and helped her push the dirt around it.

As Mandie knelt there helping Joe, she felt someone behind her. She quickly turned around to look, but there was no one in sight.

Sallie saw her reaction, and she, too, looked around. She didn't see anyone, either.

They looked at each other in silent understanding. Then there was the noise of a twig snapping in the nearby bushes. Joe and Dr. Plumbley heard it, too.

"Must be an animal or something," Mandie said, breaking the silence.

"I do not think so," Sallie said, still watching the bushes behind them. She stood up and Snowball escaped from her arms, bounding off into the bushes.

Mandie turned to chase him. "Snowball, come back here!" she called as she and Sallie followed the kitten into the bushes.

Joe and Dr. Plumbley went on with their work. Mandie bent down to look beneath the bushes. Suddenly she came upon a pair of worn boots in front of her. She raised up and came face to face with the man who was camping out at the old farmhouse. He looked wild, and his rifle was pointed straight at her.

"I done told y'all to stay away from here. I'm staking a claim," he told her in a slurred voice.

"We didn't go near your house on the rock pile," Mandie told him. Slowly backing up toward the area where Joe and Dr. Plumbley were working, she bumped into Sallie, who had been close behind her.

They grabbed each other's hands and tried to move backward, but the bushes were too thick. They got tangled in weeds and briars.

"I done told y'all to stay away from here," the man repeated. "I'm staking a claim."

Sallie whispered in Mandie's ear. "He has been drinking spirits."

Mandie was really frightened then. People sometimes went crazy like that. "We'll go, mister. We're going right now. I've lost my kitten, but as soon as we find him, we'll leave," she promised.

He just stood there pointing the rifle at them. Then suddenly he screamed in pain. Snowball had run up his back and was sticking his claws through the man's clothes. The man turned and twisted, trying to reach the kitten on his back.

The girls couldn't run away and leave the kitten.

Mandie began to yell. "Help, Joe! Help quick!"

"Help!" Sallie hollered.

Instantly Joe and Dr. Plumbley came running through the bushes.

Joe recognized the man and realized what was going on. Jumping behind the man, he grabbed the rifle. Then Dr. Plumbley knocked the man down with his fist.

"What are you doing here?" Joe demanded, holding the rifle over the man.

"Who are you, mister?" Dr. Plumbley asked.

The man didn't answer but lay there rubbing his jaw.

Snowball, frightened with all the commotion, ran to his mistress. Mandie picked him up and held him tightly.

"He's the man who was camping out in the old house on the rock pile," Joe explained. Glaring down at the man, he demanded, "I asked you a question, mister. What are you doing here?"

"I wanta know what y'all doin' on my land," the man said, managing to get to his feet.

"This is not your land," Joe told him.

"Yes it is, too," the man insisted. "Been abandoned by the Shaws all these years. I done staked a claim on it. Y'all git off my land."

"Mister, you had better get one thing straight," Dr. Plumbley said, shaking his fist in the man's face. "This is not your land and never has been, and if you don't get off of it in about one minute, I'll bust you good next time."

The man, who was much smaller than the doctor, began to tremble. "I'll go," he said, "but I'll need my rifle. I can't live without it to hunt with."

Joe held the gun tighter. "If I give you back the rifle, you'll shoot us all."

"I won't harm you," the man promised.

"You just get out of here," Dr. Plumbley ordered. "We'll take your rifle over to the boardinghouse when we get ready to leave. You can pick it up there. Now go, man!"

"I'm goin'. I'm goin' right now," the man mumbled. He turned and stumbled into the bushes.

"He had been drinking, hadn't he?" Mandie asked Joe as they walked back to the area where they were digging up bushes.

"He sure smelled like it. Ugh!" Joe made a nasty face. "But that cat . . ."

"It wasn't Snowball's fault this time," Mandie protested, hugging her kitten. "I know he ran away, but Sallie and I both felt someone watching us. That man was already there."

"Yes, the kitten may have saved your lives by attacking that man," Dr. Plumbley agreed. "He is one smart cat."

"Well, anyhow, we'd better get on with our work," Joe said, reaching for a bush to put back into place.

Once more Snowball escaped from Mandie's arms and ran straight to the hole and started scratching, throwing dirt all over Joe.

"Hey, Mandie, get that cat out of the way!" Joe hollered.

"All right." Mandie hurried to pick up Snowball. The kitten tried to resist her. "I'm sorry he kicked dirt all over you, Joe." She looked down at the hole he was going to put the bush in and blinked.

"Wait!" she cried. Stooping down beside the hole, she dug at the dirt with her hand. "There's something here!"

Joe quickly picked up the hoe and removed more dirt. Sallie and Dr. Plumbley crowded in to see what was going on.

With a clank, the hoe struck something. Joe dropped the tool and swept the dirt away with his hand, uncovering the top of a ceramic jar.

"We've found it! We've found it!" Mandie jumped up and down.

"Yes, we have!" Sallie exclaimed.

Dr. Plumbley wiped the perspiration from his face. "Thank goodness!" he said.

Joe carefully pulled the jar from the hole in the ground. It came out whole except for the bottom, which had cracked off. He gently laid the jar down in front of Mandie. Everyone sat down to see what it was.

Mandie dusted off the dirt. "A cookie jar!"

"Be careful. It's broken," Sallie cautioned.

Removing the lid, Mandie pulled out a faded piece of paper, which was wedged inside the jar.

Joe watched breathlessly as Mandie unfolded the paper. "I'll just give up if that's another map telling us to go somewhere else," he moaned.

The handwriting was dim, and the paper was crumbling. They all leaned over it as Mandie read aloud, " 'Hezekiah and his grandparents are so poor. I know my father helps them, but I want to do my share, too.' "

Mandie looked up at the doctor in amazement.

"Keep reading," Joe urged.

Mandie continued. " 'Hezekiah wants to grow up and become a doctor, and I think he would make a good one I want to help him. My father has so much money. We need to give a lot of it away. I found this ruby myself in my father's mine. Hezekiah wouldn't be able to get his education here in the South, but the ruby must be worth enough money to pay for a doctor's education in New York City. So I'll hide it here until Hezekiah is old enough to go up North and learn to be a doctor. "For unto whom

soever much is given, of him shall be much required."
Luke 12:48.' " Mandie's voice broke as she finished reading.

Tears flowed down Dr. Plumbley's black face. Everyone was silent for a moment.

"But where is the ruby?" Joe asked.

Mandie bent to look into the hole in the ground.
Something glittered in the sunlight which filtered through
the trees. She reached down and lifted the bottom of the
ceramic jar, which held a huge ruby.

Mandie trembled as she reached for Dr. Plumbley's
hand and tried to press the ruby into it. Her blue eyes
clouded with tears. "It's yours, Hezekiah," she whispered
hoarsely.

"No, no, Missy," the doctor protested. He pushed the
stone back into her hand. "I can't take that."

"But it was Ruby's, and she wanted to give it to you,"
Mandie said, still offering the ruby to him. "I wish you
could have had it before now to pay for your education."

"It would not have been possible for me to take it
back then, either, Missy," he explained. "That is too valuable for someone to give away. You must give it to your
uncle." He took a handkerchief out of his pocket to wipe
his eyes.

"But it's not my uncle's," Mandie insisted. "It was Ruby's. She said in the note that she found it herself and
that she was saving it for you. You have to take it, please."

"Missy, I don't want to argue about it. Let's just give it
to your uncle and let him decide what to do with it," the
doctor said.

"I know what he'll decide," Mandie said. "He'll do what
Ruby planned to do with it. I'll give it to him and you'll
see."

Dr. Plumbley rose and went back to working. "If we hurry and get those bushes replanted, I might get back in time for supper with Abraham," he said.

"Don't worry about supper," Mandie told him. "If it's too late to eat with Abraham, I'm sure my Uncle John will ask you to eat with us. And Jenny cooks wonderful meals."

Dr. Plumbley stopped for a moment. "What are we going to do about Jenny and Abraham?" he asked. "Do y'all have any suggestions about how we can get those two silly fools back together? They are absolutely wasting their lives by staying angry with each other."

"If they have been angry for forty years, I do not see a chance to bring them back together," Sallie said.

"Maybe we could work on Jenny if you would work on Abraham, Dr. Plumbley," Mandie suggested. "He's your friend, and he might listen to you."

"I don't know," the doctor said. "We've known each other ever since we were born, I suppose. But even though we did stay in touch through the mail, we've been separated a good many years. And Abraham's always been stubborn."

Joe helped the doctor replant another bush. "Why don't we just tell them both what we think of them for their childish nonsense?" he said. "I believe in coming out with it, whatever it may be."

"I would think that might cause them to become more stubborn if we criticized them," Sallie cautioned.

"We could try. If that didn't work, we could think up something else," Mandie said. "Maybe Uncle John knows more about it than Abraham told us."

"Yes, let's do talk to your uncle," the doctor agreed. "This worries me because I think so much of Abraham."

"My grandfather probably knows all about it, but he never tells any of his secrets unless he is forced to," Sallie reminded them.

"He might tell us something about this situation," Dr. Plumbley said.

Joe stepped back and surveyed their work. "Looks good as new again," he announced. "I don't think we harmed the plants any."

"I think they will be all right," said Dr. Plumbley. "Now, we must take the rifle back to the boardinghouse."

"I forgot about that," Joe groaned. "And here I am, starving to death." He picked up the rifle where he had laid it.

"I'm anxious to show the ruby to Uncle John and Mother." Mandie held Snowball tightly as she put the ruby and the note in her pocket.

Dr. Plumbley picked up the hoe. "I'll carry this," he offered.

Heading back the way they had come, they crossed the road again and went inside the boardinghouse. Jud Jenkinson stood behind the counter in the store.

"Well, hello, young folks. Glad to see you again," he greeted them.

Mandie introduced Dr. Plumbley. "He lived in the house that burned down here before yours was built. His grandparents died in that fire."

Jud came out from behind the counter to shake hands with the doctor. "I'm pleased to make your acquaintance," he said. "Do you still live around here, Doctor?"

"No, I've been in New York ever since my grandparents died," Dr. Plumbley replied. "I have my own medical practice up there. I'm just visiting my brother, Elijah Plumbley. He lives about ten miles down the main road from town."

"I believe I've heard of him," Jud said. "If you've been gone all these years, you probably found everything a lot different here in Franklin."

"Just about everything." Dr. Plumbley laughed.

"We've come to ask a favor, Mr. Jenkinson," Joe said, laying the rifle on the counter. "This belongs to a wild man who says he's staking a claim to that old house on the rock pile across the road a ways. He threatened us with the gun for being on the land." Joe's voice squeaked a little. "We managed to take the gun away from him, and we told him we'd leave it here. Would you mind giving it to him if he comes looking for it?"

"Why, I'll be glad to," Mr. Jenkinson agreed. "But if you're talking about property within three miles of here across the road, it all belongs to the Shaws. Didn't you know that, Miss Mandie?"

"No, I don't know anything about Uncle John's property," Mandie answered. "But Hezekiah—Dr. Plumbley here—said it used to be my grandfather's."

The man nodded.

"Thanks, Mr. Jenkinson," Joe said. "We have to be going now. That delicious smell of food from your kitchen makes me hungry, and it'll be suppertime by the time we get back to Mandie's house."

"You're welcome. Y'all come back to see me," Mr. Jenkinson called to them as they left.

Mandie set Snowball on her shoulder. "Now we have three things to ask Uncle John about," she said: "the ruby, this crazy man, and Jenny and Abraham."

They hurried along the dirt path back to Uncle John's house.

"I hope he has all the answers," Joe said.

"If he does not know, my grandfather will know all about those things," Sallie promised.

"If he'll tell," Mandie added.

Chapter 11 / Other People's Business

"We found it! We found it!" the three young people cried, rushing into the Shaws' sunroom.

Uncle John, Elizabeth, and Uncle Ned halted their conversation abruptly.

"Look!" Mandie put Snowball down and hurriedly took the huge ruby out of her apron pocket. "This is what we found!" she exclaimed. "And here's the note that was buried with it." She handed the ruby and the paper to Uncle John.

The young people dropped into chairs around the room, and Dr. Plumbley sat on the settee with Uncle John and Elizabeth.

John Shaw quickly scanned the note and examined the ruby. Elizabeth read the note aloud so Uncle Ned would know what was going on. A sad expression crossed Uncle Ned's wrinkled face.

"Imagine, burying a ruby like this!" Elizabeth examined the gem, then gave it back to her husband.

"Dr. Plumbley, I believe you have just inherited what looks like a perfect ruby," John said, offering the ruby to the doctor.

Dr. Plumbley shook his head. "Oh, no, Mr. Shaw. I couldn't accept that. It wouldn't be right of me."

"Oh, nonsense!" John replied. "It plainly says here that Ruby was saving it for you. I'd like to carry out her wishes. If she had lived, I'm sure you would have had it long before now. And if my father had known about it, he would have made sure that you got it before he died."

"But Mr. Shaw, Ruby wanted to keep that for my education. Like I told these young people, I got my education years ago, and I've long since repaid my aunt who financed it. I don't need it now," the doctor insisted.

"That doesn't matter. It is yours. Ruby gave it to you. There was just a delay in your receiving it," John said, once again holding the ruby out to him.

Dr. Plumbley stood up. "I'm afraid I must be going now," he said. "Abraham is supposed to have supper ready for me. It has been a pleasure meeting all you good folks, and I hope to see you again."

"Wait, Dr. Plumbley." Mandie stood up, trying to detain him. "We haven't decided what we're going to do about Jenny and Abraham, remember?"

"And we haven't told Mr. Shaw about the crazy man yet," Joe added.

Sallie glanced at her grandfather. "Yes, we must discuss this while my grandfather is also present," she said. "He may know something."

The doctor looked into Mandie's pleading blue eyes and sat back down. "I can only stay a minute longer, or Abraham will think I'm not coming back," the doctor insisted.

Mandie returned to her chair. "First, we'll tell them about the crazy man," she began, relating their adventures with the wild man and his rifle.

Elizabeth's face showed alarm, and Uncle Ned leaned forward in concern.

"You didn't find out who the man was?" Uncle John asked with a frown.

"No, he wouldn't tell us his name," Mandie replied.

"We were so afraid of him we wanted to hurry and get away," Sallie said.

"I'm pretty sure he had been drinking," Joe explained. "He was wild. He didn't make any sense."

"He could have been dangerous," Uncle John said. "We do still own that land and also that old house sitting on the rock pile. We just haven't used it in a long time. He had no right to be on our land. There's no way he can claim it."

Uncle Ned finally spoke. "Must be man named Sod. Live in Burningtown."

"Sod?" Uncle John questioned the odd name. "I've never heard of him."

Dr. Plumbley turned to Uncle Ned. "Was his father named Lister?"

Uncle Ned nodded. "Yes, father dead long ago."

"I thought there was something familiar about him. He's about the same age I am. I remember he was always stirring up trouble among the young people," Dr. Plumbley told them. "Back then people thought he had a little something missing."

"I think I know whom you're talking about," John said. "I wonder why he thinks he can stake a claim to our property?"

"He have more missing now. Make no sense," Uncle Ned observed.

"Maybe he has also become a drunkard," Dr. Plumbley suggested. "Anyway, I think we're rid of him. I don't believe he'll be back."

"I'm glad Dr. Plumbley was with y'all," Elizabeth said. "He could have hurt you."

"Uncle John, we have something else we want to talk to you about," Mandie said, changing the subject. "Did you know that Abraham and Jenny are married?"

Uncle John nodded slowly and smiled at her.

"And that they haven't lived together in forty years?" Mandie continued.

Uncle John kept nodding. "Yes, we know all about that."

"John!" Elizabeth sounded shocked. "You mean our cook, Jenny, is married to Abraham the gardener? Why does she live here in the house with us while he stays in that cottage in the back yard? What happened?"

Mandie related what Abraham had said about the man at the stables, but Elizabeth couldn't believe the story.

"Well, I've never heard of such a silly reason to separate," Elizabeth said. "And this has been going on for forty years?"

Sallie sat up straight in her chair. "I think he is still in love with Jenny," she said.

Uncle Ned nodded. "Too stubborn to tell her."

"You're right, Uncle Ned," John Shaw agreed. "Abraham has always been a stubborn man. He always has to have things his way. My father let him run the garden whatever way he wanted to. He does a good job if you leave him alone, but don't ever tell him he's wrong about anything, especially about Jenny."

"What about Jenny?" Mandie asked. "Is she stubborn, too?"

"Well, sometimes," Uncle John said. "But you can get her to see two sides of a question most of the time."

"Then maybe we should work on her," Joe said.

Elizabeth's eyebrows shot up. "Work on her?"

"We've all decided to see if we can get them together again," Mandie said.

"Dear, don't go interfering in other's people's business," Elizabeth warned.

"We're only trying to help," Mandie replied.

"We think if one knows how the other one feels, we might be able to make them realize they're wasting their lives apart," Joe explained.

"And make them realize that they do still love each other," Sallie added.

Uncle Ned smiled. "Pray Big God help. Been tried before."

"Tried before, Uncle Ned?" Mandie asked.

"I try. Listen, but do nothing," the old Indian replied. "Too stubborn."

Dr. Plumbley stood up again. "I really must go. Abraham is probably waiting for me to eat with him."

"Won't you please take this ruby?" Uncle John tried again, standing up beside the big man. "It's rightfully yours. And it would give me great pleasure to be able to carry out Ruby's wishes."

"No, thank you, Mr. Shaw, but I couldn't accept such a gift," the doctor told him. "I appreciate your kindness, and I hope we remain friends."

"Of course we'll always be friends," Uncle John assured him. "This has nothing to do with our friendship. We want you to feel welcome at our house here at any time."

"Yes, Dr. Plumbley, you must come back to visit us," Elizabeth insisted. "It is our good fortune to know a friend of John's sister, Ruby."

"Thank you, ma'am," the doctor said. "Thank you very much. I will come again. And if y'all are ever up in New York, please let me know, and come to visit with my wife and me."

Mandie's blue eyes lit up. "Uncle John, could we go to New York one day?" she asked. "I've never been there."

Uncle John smiled down at her. "One of these days we'll just have to take a trip up there," he said.

Dr. Plumbley turned to go.

"When are you leaving town, Dr. Plumbley?" Joe asked.

"If my brother is getting along as well tomorrow morning as he has been, I plan to return to New York tomorrow," the doctor said. "I have enjoyed being with you young people especially."

"Thank you, sir," Joe said.

"We've enjoyed getting to know you, Hezekiah," Mandie said. She took his hand and gave it a squeeze.

The Negro doctor smiled with a sad expression in his eyes.

"Will you talk to Abraham?" Sallie asked.

"Yes, I will talk to him. You young people work on Jenny," he said, leaving the room. "Good night and thanks."

After seeing the doctor to the front door, Uncle John returned to the sunroom and sat down. He turned the ruby over in his hands. "What am I going to do with this?" he asked, looking at Uncle Ned.

"Maybe Elijah, brother of Samuel, need," the old Indian suggested.

"That's an idea. We'll find out what his circumstances are and see if we can help him," John agreed.

"Ruby would be disappointed if she knew Hezekiah

wouldn't accept the ruby, wouldn't she?" Mandie said.

"I imagine so." Uncle John nodded. "I just wish there were some way to get him to take it."

"Ruby must have had a very warm heart to have given him something so valuable," Elizabeth remarked.

Uncle Ned smiled sadly. "Ruby good all way through," he said.

"Maybe we can figure out some way to carry out Ruby's wishes," Mandie suggested.

"But what about Jenny?" Joe asked.

Mandie walked over to her mother and put her arm around her. "Mother, is Jenny cooking supper right now?" she asked.

"Well, not exactly cooking. Since this is Sunday, she's probably warming up what was left over from our noon meal," Elizabeth replied.

"Let's go see what she's doing," Mandie told Joe and Sallie.

The three young people rose and started to leave the room.

"All of you get washed up first, so you'll be ready to eat," Elizabeth told them.

They hurried upstairs, hastily cleaned up, and raced back down to the kitchen, where Jenny was stirring two pots of food at once on the big iron cookstove. Jenny saw them come in and quickly turned back to the stove.

Joe strode up behind her, trying to look into the pots. "Jenny, something smells delicious!" he exclaimed.

"Git out of here," she snapped. "I ain't got no time fo' no foolishness."

"What we want to talk to you about is not foolishness. It's just plain common sense," Mandie said.

The cook didn't reply. She just kept stirring the pots.

"Jenny, this food smells awfully good," Joe complimented her. "Why don't you take some of this nice-smelling food to poor old Abraham out there all alone in his little house?"

"Git!" Jenny hissed.

"We don't want to git," Mandie told her. "We want to stay right here and talk to you until you get supper on the table."

"Well, you ain't, Missy," Jenny said, turning to look at her, " 'cause I'll go git Aunt Lou to git you out of here."

"You don't want Aunt Lou to hear what we're going to talk to you about, do you?" Joe asked.

"Ain't nuthin' to talk 'bout," Jenny said, still stirring the pots.

"I don't think there's been enough talking done. That's what's wrong with things now," Mandie said. "If you and Abraham had really talked things over, you wouldn't be living here alone in the house and him alone out there in the little cottage."

"Ain't none of yo' bidness." Jenny slammed a lid onto one of the pots.

"We're only trying to help you," Mandie insisted.

Sallie looked directly into Jenny's eyes. "Abraham still loves you," she said.

Jenny stopped stirring.

"He does," Sallie assured her.

Jenny slammed the lid onto another pot and said, "No, he don't!"

"But he does still love you a whole lot, Jenny," Mandie argued.

"Now how y'all knows dat?" Jenny asked.

Joe smiled. "We have ways of finding out things."

"What ways dat be?" Jenny asked.

"We talked to Abraham," Mandie said.

"And he done tol' you dat?"

"He didn't have to say it," Mandie said. "We could tell."

Just then one of the pots on the stove started to boil over. Jenny quickly turned back to the stove and slid the pot off the burner. "Y'all gwine t' cause me t' burn up de supper, and den you won't have nuthin' t' eat tonight," she grumbled.

"We'll help you watch it," Joe said. Picking up a large spoon, he began stirring one of the pots. "Oh, Jenny, these beans are starting to stick." He grabbed a towel nearby and pulled the pot off the burner.

Mandie tried to get back to the subject. "Jenny, don't you love Abraham?" she asked. "You must have loved him when you married him."

Jenny turned around and put her hands on her slim hips. "Y'all git out of here," she demanded, "or y'all ain't gwine t' have no supper."

"You might as well give in," Joe teased. "It's three against one."

Jenny busied herself at the stove again. "Go ahaid and talk. You ain't gittin' no answers."

"Didn't you take the vows, 'till death do us part,' when you married Abraham?" Mandie persisted. "You're not living up to your part of the bargain."

"And don't blame it all on Abraham," Joe added.

"Maybe there were some misunderstandings on both sides," Mandie added.

Jenny kept stirring the pots vigorously.

"Everybody has faults," Mandie reminded her. "Nobody is perfect. So we need to forgive each other and wipe the slate clean."

Sallie rested her hand lightly on Jenny's shoulder. "Abraham is so lonely out there in that little cottage all alone," she said softly. "He does not even have anyone to talk to out there."

Jenny glanced at the Indian girl.

"Really lonely," Sallie added.

Silently, Jenny began removing the pots from the stove. Joe rushed to help her, and then she started taking dishes down from the cupboard.

"And you must be lonely all alone up there in that little room," Mandie said. "It's just not right for a man and his wife to be separated."

Jenny slammed the dishes down, but fortunately they didn't break. She turned quickly to face Mandie. "You listen here now! It better a man and his wife live apart than to live together and fuss and fight!" she said vehemently.

"Did y'all fuss and fight?" Mandie asked, taken aback.

"It was all one-sided fussin' wid dat Abraham doin' it all," Jenny replied. "I wouldn't belittle myself to fuss back. I jes' up and left."

"Then we'll have to talk to Abraham," Joe said.

"Don't do no good to talk to dat man. Too stubborn," Jenny said, taking down more dishes.

"That is what my grandfather said—that Abraham is stubborn," Sallie confirmed.

Mandie smoothed her blonde braid. "We'll have to find a way to break his stubborn streak."

"Den y'all go do dat and leave me alone," Jenny told them.

The three young people looked at each other and smiled. Maybe Jenny was listening to them after all.

"Let's run over there and see what Abraham is doing," Mandie suggested.

"Fine," Joe agreed. "As long as we get back in time for supper."

"Supper be ready in a minute," Jenny warned them.

"We'll hurry," Mandie said.

They rushed out the back door and over to Abraham's little cottage.

Abraham came to the door and allowed them to come back to the kitchen where he and Dr. Plumbley were preparing their supper. "What y'all be wantin'?" he fussed.

"We want to see Dr. Plumbley for a minute," Mandie said. She stood on tiptoe to speak into the doctor's ear. "We've been talking to you-know-who," she whispered.

Dr. Plumbley nodded and continued setting the table.

Mandie turned to the gardener. "Abraham, we've been talking to Jenny, and we found out she still loves you," Mandie said.

Abraham turned furiously, burning his finger on a pot handle. "It dat's what y'all come here fo'," he yelled, "y'all kin jes' git back to de big house!" He stuck his finger in his mouth to cool the burn.

"That food smells good, Abraham. You must be a good cook," Joe said.

Abraham ignored the compliment.

"Jenny sure is a good cook, too," Joe continued. "The Shaws are lucky people to have her to cook all those delicious meals. She sure knows what she's doing."

"She don't know what she's doin'," Abraham argued. "She don't know how to come in outta de rain."

"She must know something about what she's doing because she sure cooks good meals. We enjoy them," Mandie said.

"And she does still love you, Abraham," Sallie assured him.

"Love!" the gardener scoffed. "Dat woman don't know what dat word mean!"

Mandie sighed deeply. "Abraham, did Dr. Plumbley tell you about what we found this afternoon?" she asked. "You should have come with us."

"No, he ain't told me what you found," Abraham said. "You mean y'all done found sumpin'?"

"We found Ruby's treasure on the map we showed you. It was a great big ruby, a real one," Mandie explained.

"A great big ruby? What you gwine to do wid it?" Abraham asked.

"Ruby left a note that said she wanted Dr. Plumbley to have it, and Uncle John tried to give it to him, but he wouldn't take it," Mandie replied.

Abraham whirled to face his doctor friend. "Wouldn't take it?" he hollered. "Is you crazy in de haid? Why don't you take dat ruby?"

Dr. Plumbley looked up from dishing food from the pot. "I explained to Mr. Shaw that I don't need it," he said.

"Well, he don't need it neither," Abraham said. "Anybody offer me anything like dat, I takes it."

Mandie smiled at the doctor. "I don't think Abraham is the only stubborn one around here."

"Me stubborn?" Abraham protested. "I ain't stubborn."

"You are definitely stubborn, Abraham," Mandie told him. "You're so stubborn you'd rather live alone than go tell Jenny you still love her."

Abraham thought for a moment. "She don't love me," he said. "She never did."

"You're not a mind reader," Dr. Plumbley spoke up.

"How do you know what Jenny thinks? You've never asked her, have you?"

"I don't hafta aks her. I knows," Abraham muttered as he set a platter of fried chicken on the table.

"No, you don't know either. You're guessing," the doctor argued.

There was a knock at the door and Liza yelled, "Eatin' time! Eatin' time!"

"Coming!" Joe yelled back.

"We'll see you later, Abraham," Mandie said. "Good night, Dr. Plumbley."

The three young people hurried back to the house for their supper. As they entered the back door they came face to face with Aunt Lou.

Aunt Lou shook her big apron at them. "Y'all git in dat dinin' room," she scolded. "And don't y'all come botherin' de cook no mo'. You hear?"

"We won't," they all promised.

They met up with the adults in the hallway on their way into the dining room.

"I hear y'all have been in the kitchen bothering Jenny," Elizabeth chided. "I suppose you have also been bothering Abraham."

After Uncle John returned thanks for the food at the table, Liza placed a platter of food in front of them. "Oh, dat botherin' done Jenny good," she said. "She be in there singin' a love song. I ain't never seen her so happy."

The three young people looked at one another and grinned.

"She sho' is, and I ain't never heerd her sing like dat befo'," the Negro girl continued. "I don't know what's goin' on, but it sho' be good."

Chapter 12 / Much Is Given

Before sunrise Monday morning, the young people gathered in the sunroom, waiting for Jenny to prepare breakfast. Snowball didn't like the early hour, and he curled up asleep by his mistress.

Sallie sat down beside Mandie on the settee. "We must part ways today," she said sadly.

"But we can all get together for Christmas," Joe reminded her. "And that's not so long off."

"I feel as though our search was all for nothing," Mandie said with a little pout. "Dr. Plumbley won't take the ruby, and Uncle John doesn't know what to do with it."

"He'll come up with a good use for it, I'm sure," Joe said.

The young people sat silently for several moments, then Mandie spoke. "Do you reckon Abraham and Jenny will ever get together again?"

"They might if they would talk things over," Sallie said.

"But they're not even at the talking stage," Joe remarked. "They don't want to talk to each other."

"I just thought of something." Mandie changed the subject. "We promised to let Mrs. Hadley know what we found buried on the map."

"Would we have time to visit them this morning?" Sallie asked. "I do not know what time my grandfather and I will be leaving. Maybe he would ride out there with us this morning."

"My father probably won't be here until this afternoon. He has some calls to make on the way," Joe said.

"I'll ask my mother if we can go," Mandie promised.

When Elizabeth and Uncle John came downstairs for breakfast, they gave the young people permission to visit the Hadleys, provided Uncle Ned went with them. He agreed to go.

Uncle John had put the ruby away in his safe because it was too valuable for Mandie to be carrying around. But he allowed her to take the note they had found to show Mrs. Hadley.

When they arrived, they joined the Hadleys in their parlor. Mrs. Hadley read the note and listened to the three young people's account of what they found.

"What a sad story," the woman responded.

"If only we could get Dr. Plumbley to accept the ruby," Mandie said.

Mrs. Hadley gave the note back to Mandie. "But dear, you said he told y'all he didn't need it."

"My Uncle John doesn't need it either," Mandie replied.

"Think of all the good that could be done with that ruby," the woman mused. "It could feed a lot of hungry people or pay for medical treatment of sick people who can't afford a doctor, especially the Cherokees."

"We're building a hospital for the Cherokees not far from where Uncle Ned and Sallie live," Mandie told her. "We were exploring a cave and found some gold that belonged to them many years ago. They wouldn't accept the gold, so we're using it to build the hospital."

"That's a wonderful thing to do," said Mr. Hadley, who was sitting next to Uncle Ned. "So many people can't afford a doctor these days."

"My father doctors sick people whether they can pay or not," Joe spoke up. "He says God gave him his talents in medicine and that they should be put to use for the good of the people, not just for profit."

"Dr. Woodard is a fine man," Mr. Hadley said. "Are you going to study medicine, too, when you grow up?"

"No, sir, I don't think so," Joe replied. "I think I'd rather be a lawyer."

"Well, people need lawyers, too," Mrs. Hadley agreed.

Uncle Ned stood up. "Must go now," he announced.

The young people promised to visit again and rode off on their ponies with Uncle Ned.

As they approached the Shaw home, they spotted Dr. Plumbley's horse and buggy at the gate.

Mandie frowned in confusion. "I didn't think Dr. Plumbley was coming back again," she said. "I thought he was going home to New York."

"Maybe he forgot something," Sallie suggested.

"Probably came by to tell Abraham good-bye," Joe said.

They all dismounted and tied their horses to the hitching post at the gate.

"When are we leaving to go home, my grandfather?" Sallie asked.

"Eat first, then go," Uncle Ned said, starting up the walkway to the house.

The young people rushed ahead. Inside, they met Liza in the front hallway.

"In de parlor," she said, waving her hand in that direction.

They could hear Dr. Plumbley's strong voice and hurried to see why he had come back. Stopping at the doorway, with Uncle Ned behind them, they looked into the parlor.

Uncle John and Elizabeth sat on the settee. Dr. Plumbley was seated nearby. A tall, thin Negro boy, a little older than Joe, sat alone by a window.

"Come on in. This is Dr. Plumbley's brother's grandson, Moses," Uncle John said, introducing everyone.

The young people sat down near Moses.

"I thought you were leaving town this morning," Mandie said to Dr. Plumbley.

The doctor drew a deep breath. "I had planned to," he said. "But my brother Elijah crossed over in his sleep sometime during the night."

"He died?" Mandie gasped. "Oh, I'm sorry, Dr. Plumbley."

Joe and Sallie also expressed their sympathy.

"I thought he was better," Dr. Plumbley said, wiping his eyes with a handkerchief, "but I reckon the Lord thought it was time for him to go."

Moses caught his breath and looked away from the young people so they wouldn't see the tears in his eyes.

"Is there anything we can do?" Joe asked.

"No, thank you," the doctor replied. "I just came to town to make the arrangements. I'll be leaving as soon as everything is over. Moses will be alone now since both his parents are dead. So I brought him to town to see if he could stay with Abraham until I can send for him. Moses wants to study medicine."

"Why don't you take him with you when you leave?" Mandie asked.

The doctor didn't answer for a moment, and then he said, "Well, you see, it costs a lot of money to go to New York from here. And my wife and I will have to find a larger place to live. We only have one bedroom—"

"The ruby!" Mandie interrupted. "Uncle John, the ruby! We can give it to Moses!"

Uncle John smiled at her. "That's exactly what I was thinking. I'll go get it."

As he left the room, Dr. Plumbley protested. "No, no," he said. "Moses couldn't accept that ruby any more than I could."

Moses looked puzzled, and the young people explained how they came to find the ruby.

"I sho' wish I could've gone with y'all," Moses said. "Must've been a lot of fun."

"Except for the crazy man threatening us," Joe reminded him.

When Uncle John came back into the room, he walked over to Moses and showed the ruby to him. "This is what they found," he said, cradling the ruby in the palm of his hand.

Moses' eyes grew wide at the sight of the shiny red gem.

Uncle John walked over to sit beside Dr. Plumbley. "Now there's no use arguing about this," he said. "We want you to take this and use it for Moses' education. There are never enough doctors, so the money will be well spent." John held the stone out to the doctor.

"That's right," Dr. Plumbley replied. "There's no use arguing about it because we're not going to accept it." He shook his head. "There's no way we could ever pay you back, so it just wouldn't be right for us to take it."

"You could take the boy on home with you to New York now, and you wouldn't have to send for him later," John Shaw reasoned. "You could find a bigger place to live after you get him up there and put him in school."

"Mr. Shaw, you don't realize how much your family has already done for mine," Dr. Plumbley argued. "Your father practically fed and clothed my grandparents and me. And I've never been able to repay it. I can't get further indebted to the Shaw family."

"Stubborn, just like Abraham," said Uncle Ned.

"You also have the cost of your brother's funeral to pay out," John reminded him. "How do you think you're going to manage all these things without some help? You told us you only make a meager living from doctoring. This is not my help. It's Ruby helping you."

"It's not Ruby's help. She left many years ago. That stone belongs to you and nobody else," the doctor insisted.

"You're wrong. It is not mine," John replied. "I consider the note that Ruby wrote the same as a will. She willed this to you, and she would be awfully hurt if she knew you wouldn't accept it."

Dr. Plumbley stood up. "I'm sorry, Mr. Shaw. I don't look at it that way. I thank you very much, but I cannot accept the ruby. Now, I need to find Abraham and talk to him about Moses."

After the doctor and his nephew had gone, John Shaw turned to his wife. "I don't understand why he won't take this ruby," he said in frustration.

"Well, he just doesn't want it, so you can't make him accept it, John," Elizabeth said.

"I guess I should lock it up again then," John said, rising to leave the room.

Mandie looked at her friends. "Let's go outside," she suggested.

Sallie and Joe followed her out onto the front porch, and they all sat down in the big swing. For several minutes they gently rocked back and forth in the swing, talking about the ruby, Dr. Plumbley, his nephew, and the situation with Abraham and Jenny.

"Why don't we go see what Jenny is cooking for dinner?" Joe suggested. "I'm hungry."

Mandie and Sallie laughed.

"I know what you're up to, Joe Woodard," Mandie teased as they rose from the swing.

"We'd better be quiet. Aunt Lou may catch us." Joe led the way around the house to the back door, so they wouldn't have to pass the parlor, where the adults were sitting.

The three were trying to silently ease the back door open when Jenny suddenly came up behind them and pushed it open.

"Out o' my way! I'se gotta see 'bout de food befo' it burn up," Jenny fussed, rushing into the kitchen.

The three young people stood outside the back door for a moment.

"Now where has Jenny been?" Joe asked quietly.

"Probably taking the garbage out," Sallie answered.

"Or visiting Abraham?" Mandie speculated.

"Abraham? Do you think she might have been over there?" Joe asked.

"Let's go visit him," Mandie said.

They turned and walked over to the gardener's cottage, but he was nowhere to be seen. Dr. Plumbley and Moses were sitting on Abraham's porch alone.

"Is Abraham not home?" Mandie asked as she and

her two friends sat down on the steps.

"No, we're waiting for him," Dr. Plumbley replied.

"Here he comes now," Joe said.

Abraham plodded across the yard from the back door of the big house, carrying a flour sack stuffed full of something. He stumbled up onto the porch, shoved the sack through his front door, and then sat down on the porch with the doctor. "I jes' heered 'bout Elijah, Samuel. I'm terrible sorry," he said. "Mr. Shaw jes' told me."

"You weren't home when we came," Dr. Plumbley told his friend, "so we went over there."

"Ain't been gone long." Abraham slowly rocked back and forth in his rocking chair. "Been over to de big house gittin' some things."

Dr. Plumbley looked at Abraham pleadingly. "I wanted to ask you if you'd let Moses stay here with you until I can send for him," he said. "I don't want him to stay alone out there in Elijah's house."

"Stay here wid me?" Abraham stopped rocking and pondered the question.

"I'll send you money for his board, of course," Dr. Plumbley said.

"Stay wid me?" Abraham repeated. "I don't think dat would work out, Samuel."

"What do you mean, Abraham? Moses is a good boy, easy to get along with," the doctor assured him.

Abraham looked directly at the boy. "I knows you's a good boy," he said. "It's jes' dat it wouldn't be—uh—convenient—uh—right now."

"Convenient? What on earth are you talking about?" the doctor asked.

The young people leaned forward, listening for his answer.

"I—uh—already have somebody gwine t' stay wid me," Abraham explained, avoiding the doctor's gaze.

"Oh, I see. I didn't know you were taking in a boarder," Dr. Plumbley said.

"Well, dadblame it, Samuel!" Abraham exploded. "Here ebrybody been preachin' to me, and when I finally gits 'round to askin' Jenny to come home, you be tryin' to give me a boarder. She wouldn't like dat."

"Abraham!" Mandie cried. "Jenny is coming home?" She jumped up and reached for the old man's hand. "I'm thrilled to death!"

"Abraham, if your wife is coming back to live with you, I wouldn't interfere with that for anything in the world." Dr. Plumbley beamed. "I'm so happy for you!"

"Let's go see Jenny!" Joe exclaimed.

The young people hurried across the yard to the big house, but as they pushed open the back door, they came face to face with Aunt Lou.

"Where y'all goin' in sech a all-fired hurry?" Aunt Lou demanded.

"We've got to see Jenny, Aunt Lou," Mandie answered.

The big Negro housekeeper quickly grabbed her by the shoulders and turned her the other direction. "You ain't botherin' Jenny. She got to git dat dinnuh done!" Aunt Lou scolded. "Now git goin'."

"But we just wanted to tell her how happy we are that she is moving in with Abraham," Mandie said.

"I knows all 'bout dat," Aunt Lou said. "You tell her later."

Mandie sighed, and she and her friends walked down the hallway to the parlor, where the adults still sat talking.

"Guess what?" Mandie announced. "Jenny is moving in with Abraham."

"That's great," Uncle John replied.

"It's about time," Elizabeth agreed.

Uncle Ned grinned broadly.

"But it's not all good news," Joe said. "Abraham is not going to let Moses stay with him because Jenny won't like it."

Everyone became silent, and the three young people sat down on the settee.

"I wonder what Dr. Plumbley is going to do," Sallie said.

"He is going to have to take that ruby, whether he likes it or not," Mandie stated.

Uncle John smiled. "You're right, Amanda," he agreed. "You get him back in here while I go get the ruby."

The young people hurried over to Abraham's front porch where Abraham, Dr. Plumbley, and Moses were still sitting.

"Uncle John wants you to come back to see him for a minute, Dr. Plumbley," Mandie called up to the porch.

"Do you know what he wants? We have to be going," the doctor replied.

"He just said to ask you to come back for a minute," Mandie said. "Come on."

Dr. Plumbley and Moses followed the young people to the house and into the parlor where John Shaw sat holding the ruby once more.

"You wanted to see us about something, Mr. Shaw?" Dr. Plumbley asked.

"Yes, sit down for just a minute. I know you're in a hurry," John Shaw told him.

Everyone sat down.

John cleared his throat. "Now there is nothing left for you to do but take this ruby for Moses," he insisted. "I understand Abraham is moving Jenny in over there and can't keep the boy."

Dr. Plumbley immediately stood up. "I'm sorry, Mr. Shaw. I've already told you I couldn't do that," the doctor refused.

John also stood. "What other alternative do you have?"

"I'll figure out something, but I can't accept charity," the doctor said.

"Charity!" John bellowed. "This is something that rightfully belongs to you!"

The doctor touched Moses on the shoulder and turned toward the door.

Mandie blocked his way. "Dr. Plumbley," she said firmly, "are you going to let your pride stand in the way of Moses' education? There have been plenty of other people who have paid for someone else's education before. Why can't you take the ruby for Moses? My father used to say, 'pride goeth before a fall.' "

Dr. Plumbley did not move. "I'm sorry, Missy," he said softly.

"And remember the Bible verse Ruby wrote in her note?" Mandie continued. " 'For unto whomsoever much is given, of him shall be much required.' What if your pride keeps us from living up to that?"

Tears rolled down the doctor's black face as he reached for Mandie's small hand. "Missy, you're so much like little Ruby. That's the way she always talked," he said shakily.

Mandie held her other hand out to Uncle John for the ruby, and he gave it to her. When she pressed the gem into the doctor's big hand, he didn't refuse it this time.

Dr. Plumbley stared at it through his tears. "*I* may not live that long, but *Moses* will repay this," he promised, looking at the boy. "It will all be repaid."

"You don't pay someone back for a gift," Mandie argued. "Ruby gave this to you as a gift."

"That's right," Uncle John persisted. "If you want to show your gratitude, you just help Moses be the best doctor he can be."

Just then Liza stuck her head in the door. "Dinnuh done be ready!" she announced.

Elizabeth rose gracefully. "Dr. Plumbley, you and Moses must come on in and eat dinner with us," she said. "I know you're in a hurry, but you've got to eat somewhere."

"Yes, come on," John urged.

Dr. Plumbley put his arm around Mandie. "Thank you, Missy—little Ruby." He looked up. "Thank you all for everything," he said.

As soon as the noon meal was over, Uncle Ned motioned to Mandie. "Come. Talk. Then Sallie and I leave."

She followed him out onto the front porch. The others understood and waited inside.

As they sat down in the swing, Uncle Ned took Mandie's small white hand in his. His face was shining as he spoke to her. "Papoose do good job," he said. "Ruby be proud of Papoose."

"Thank you, Uncle Ned. When you asked me to come out here, I was wondering what I had done wrong," Mandie admitted. "What you say to me always means so much."

"See? Easy to be good Papoose," Uncle Ned told her. "Easy to be good as it is to be bad."

"I'm trying hard, Uncle Ned," Mandie said.

"Must ask Big God take care of Moses now his father gone to happy hunting ground," the old Indian said.

"Yes, let's do." Mandie looked toward the sky, holding the old Indian's hand. "Dear God, please take care of Moses and help him to become a doctor, a good doctor, God. He's going to miss his grandpa. Thank you."

"Yes, Big God. Bless Moses," Uncle Ned asked, looking upward.

"He will," Mandie promised.

"Yes, must go now," Uncle Ned said.

Mandie looked up suddenly, hearing the sound of approaching hoofbeats.

A stranger on horseback dismounted at the gate in front of them and came up the walkway to the front porch. "Good afternoon," he said, a little out of breath. "I have a message for Miss Amanda Shaw." He offered them an envelope.

Puzzled, Mandie took it. "I'm Amanda Shaw," she replied. "Thank you." *What is this?* she wondered.

As the man left, Mandie opened the envelope and withdrew a sheet of paper. She began reading aloud. " 'Dear Amanda, I have just learned of a great mystery here in Asheville that sounds like an adventure you would enjoy. Please hurry back in time to spend the night with me so that I may tell you about it before you have to check into school. Love always, Grandmother Taft.' "

Uncle Ned patted the top of her blonde head. "Remember. Be good Papoose. Do not get in trouble. Will see you at school first full moon," he promised.

This must be something awfully exciting for Grandmother to send me a special letter like this, Mandie thought.

She could hardly wait to return to Asheville.

Cooking with Mandie!

*A*fter days and days of begging, Mandie finally convinced Aunt Lou to teach her how to cook. You know who Aunt Lou is—Mandie's Uncle John's Housekeeper. Mandie not only loved learning how to cook, but she recorded every recipe, every "do" and "don't" that they went through. And that is how this cookbook came to be.

Mandie also learned how to cook Cherokee-style from Morning Star, Uncle Ned's wife. Sallie, her granddaughter, helped translate since Morning Star doesn't speak English. Being part Cherokee, Mandie wanted to learn how her kin-people cook.

With Mandie's step-by-step instructions, you can cook and serve meals and share the experiences of girls from the turn of the century. Learn how to bake cakes and pies, do popcorn balls, make biscuits and Southern fried chicken, as well as make Indian recipes like dried apples and potato skins.

If you love the Mandie Books, you'll love to try cooking Mandie's favorite recipes!